THE CHIEF'S CATCH

CONTEMPORARY CHRISTIAN ROMANCE

FULLER FAMILY IN BRUSH CREEK ROMANCE
BOOK SIX

LIZ ISAACSON

ISBN-13: 978-1638760924

"The Lord is gracious, and full of compassion; slow to anger, and of great mercy."

Psalms 145:8

Berlin Fuller looked at herself in the mirror, Starlee standing behind her. The stylist kept running her hands through Berlin's dark blonde hair, waiting for her to give her directions.

"What are we doing today?" shouldn't be such a hard question. Especially because Caitlyn and Scotty were loitering only a few feet away, also waiting.

Berlin switched her gaze to Caitlyn's. A preschool teacher who'd taken the day off for Berlin's transformation, she lifted her eyebrows as if to say, *Go on already.*

Scotty checked her phone, smiling at the screen.

"I want a new look," Berlin said, her voice strong and probably too loud for the nearly empty salon. "Darker hair. Shorter. Make me look...different."

Berlin was tired of her current life, and she was only twenty-seven-years-old. She'd taken as many online courses in accounting that she could, finally finishing her degree a couple of years ago by leaving Brush Creek for Colorado Springs.

She'd dated a couple of guys there, but nothing had stuck. That was how she felt about every man she went out with. Like she was some sort of Teflon and they wouldn't stick around no matter what.

"Darker?" Starlee asked, still combing her fingers through Berlin's locks. "Y'know, most women want to go lighter, not darker."

"Not too short," Caitlyn said, stepping closer. "Still brushing her shoulders. But nothing she can put in a ponytail." She met Berlin's gaze with a meaningful look in her eye. "We're not doing ponytails anymore, remember?"

Starlee looked between the friends. "Is this a hair change or a life change?"

"Life," Berlin said, squaring her shoulders. She'd just had another birthday and it was so exhausting to attend the Fuller family dinners as a singleton. Sometimes she brought Caitlyn along, but now she had a boyfriend. Scotty worked up at the horse farm at the top of the canyon, and she didn't make it down during the week that often.

She put her phone in her back pocket and stepped forward to join the conversation. "We're taking her to the summer fair tonight." Scotty leaned over Berlin's shoulder, her smile wide and beautiful. She wouldn't have any trouble getting a date tonight, not after she curled her miles of dark hair and put on her rodeo makeup. The woman was a former barrel racer, and she had a new man on her arm every weekend. She claimed to like the revolving door of male attention, but Berlin had tired of it quickly.

And at this point, she just wanted a date at all. If she had to go into the empty office for another weekend in a row so she wouldn't have to stay home alone, she might paint the whole thing bright pink. And boy, would that make Wren mad....

"She's not leavin' until she has a date." Scotty giggled. "So darker. Spruced up. Berlin's doing everything different now."

Berlin's doing everything different.

The words echoed through her head. She had told her friends that, maybe in a moment of weakness. Starlee met her eyes and said, "So darker?"

Berlin nodded, her pulse skipping just a little inside her veins.

"What color are you thinking?"

"Something like Scotty's," Berlin said. "Do you think that would work?"

"I just got a new ashy black. Want to try that?"

Ashy black sounded dangerous, deadly, different.

Berlin swallowed and nodded again. She wasn't sure how easy it was to undo something like ashy black, but she suspected it wouldn't be easy.

"I'll go mix up." Starlee left before Berlin could change her mind.

And you don't want to change your mind anyway, she

reminded herself as her friends retreated to find magazines and settle in while the first leg of the transformation began.

———

HOURS LATER, with the new do, ten times more makeup than Berlin normally wore, and with the blouse Scotty had found at the only department store in town falling off her right shoulder, she slipped her feet into a pair of ankle boots.

The jean skirt was a little too tight, and Berlin wouldn't wear it in front of her mother. But her mother wouldn't be at the summer fair tonight. Heck, Berlin shouldn't even be going. Friday night at the fair was usually filled with hormonal teenagers, all looking for someone to sneak away in the dark with.

Berlin's stomach swooped. She didn't want a summer fling. She wanted to meet an interesting man, and the summer fair was the perfect place to show up with her new look.

"So we get to choose," Caitlyn said as if she hadn't reminded Berlin of their bet at least a dozen times since they'd met for breakfast that morning. She had the whole plan laid out, from the salon appointment to the fake eyelashes to the amount of time they could spend shopping.

"I know." Berlin tugged on the hem of her skirt.

"We get an hour to find an appropriate man."

Caitlyn folded her list and tucked it in her pocket. "And whoever we choose, you have to get to ask you out. That's the deal."

"All the boys are comin' down from the horse farm tonight." Scotty looked up from her phone, her smile so wide and infectious Berlin felt herself relaxing.

"I don't like cowboys," she said.

Scotty scoffed as if the idea of not liking cowboys was utterly ridiculous. "They're not all married."

Berlin pressed her lips together, the soft pink gloss Caitlyn had insisted on a bit sticky. It would do no good to argue with Scotty. Berlin had agreed to the terms of their deal, and all she could hope for was that Caitlyn would find someone more concerned about people than he was about his mare.

"All right. Let's go." Caitlyn tucked Berlin's hair behind her ear and then flipped it out again. "You look great."

Her hair was indeed an ashy black which reflected the light strangely in different situations. She liked it a lot more out in direct sunlight, but the fair would be full of fluorescent lights in shades of orange. She shuddered just thinking about what color her hair would be then.

But she couldn't stop the inevitable, and she reminded herself—again—that she wanted to do everything backward than what she normally did. After all, her previous attempts at dating had her going on a double date with a man whose last name she'd never learned, and then a forty-year-old detective who her family had disapproved of because of the fifteen-year age difference.

She'd really liked Gray, but in the end, they were just too different. On two different ends of the life spectrum. And his fourteen-year-old daughter had been a real problem.

"Remember, no one with kids," she told her friends.

"That might be hard," Caitlyn said though she'd readily agreed to it before. "And it won't matter if they're…what?" She peered at Berlin as she drove toward the park. "Under ten?"

"Under eight," Berlin said. One of her sisters had married a widower with a seven-year-old daughter, and Dawn had been brilliant at the insta-mom thing. Berlin wasn't sure she could take on a child at only age twenty-seven, and she certainly hadn't clicked with Gray's daughter. Last she'd heard, he'd started dating an older woman with a couple of teenagers herself. A pang of loneliness hit her, and she pushed Gray out of her mind.

"No cops," she told her friends as Caitlyn found a parking spot and swung the car into it.

"Oh, no," Caitlyn said. "That wasn't part of the deal. You just said no men with teenagers."

Berlin opened her mouth to argue, but Scotty squealed in a volume that could burst eardrums and launched herself out of the backseat. A couple of cowboys loitered by the fence that ran along the walking path in the park, and she threw herself at one of them. He caught her around the waist and twirled her.

The carefree nature of the exchange had Berlin swallowing back a sour jealousy she wished she could never feel again. And yet, she asked, "Who's that?" anyway.

"Him? That's Branch. Her brother. He's been in Montana for years. She said he was going to try to make it."

"Branch isn't a name," Berlin grumbled. "That's another one. Only men with real names."

Caitlyn tipped her head back and laughed. "I have no control over that."

"You know everyone in this town."

"Please. That would be *you*." Caitlyn hipped Berlin, who stumbled sideways for a step as they approached the two cowboys. Scotty made the introductions and everyone started walking toward the festivities on the other side of the lake.

Bright lights lifted into the dark night, staining the sky with light pollution, and the din of noise could be heard from hundreds of yards away.

"An hour," Caitlyn said, skipping ahead and linking her arm through Scotty's. "C'mon, girl. We have work to do before we find guys of our own."

Berlin watched them giggle and hurry ahead, leaving her with Branch and his buddy, Henry. "Drinks are on me, boys."

They were at least smart cowboys, because neither of them argued with her. Scotty had said she'd provide a way that no one else would hit on Berlin until they'd picked out her man, and apparently that came in the form of two cowboys flanking her.

She bought sodas for them and flavored lemonade for herself, and together they camped out on the edge of the fair. The scent of hot oil filled the air, along with laughter and the dinging of bells as boyfriends won stuffed animals for their girls.

Only twenty-four minutes later—Berlin may have put a timer on her phone—Caitlyn and Scotty came pushing through the crowd.

"Got 'im." Caitlyn drew in a big breath, her chest heaving. Whether from excitement or because she needed to spend a bit more time on the treadmill, Berlin wasn't sure.

Her stomach coiled and recoiled, getting ready to strike like an angry snake. She took one more gulp of the sour lemonade and said, "Okay. I can do this."

Scotty gripped her shoulders with both hands and looked right into Berlin's eyes. "You *can* do this. Different. Dark." She giggled again and glanced at Caitlyn. "You're going to *love* him."

"I just have to get him to ask me out," Berlin said. No one had said anything about falling in love, though Berlin yearned to do that. Have someone to hold hands with, whisper secrets to, fall into a kiss with the way her sisters did.

She drew in a deep breath and said, "Point him out."

Caitlyn and Scotty turned back to the crowd, slipping to Berlin's side and pushing the cowboys out. "He's not a cowboy," Caitlyn said. "So don't let the hat fool you." She pointed toward the milk bottles. "There he is. Black hat."

Berlin scanned the crowd, but there were literally a dozen black hatted men near the milk bottles. Her heart pitted and patted and hopped around like a frog on caffeine.

"Police uniform," Scotty added. "Oh, he just laughed."

Berlin's heart sank all the way to her cute little boots. "The Chief of Police?" She turned toward Caitlyn. "You want me to get Cole Fairbanks to ask me out?"

"He's perfect for you," Caitlyn purred, giving her a little shove.

Berlin's jaw tightened and she gave a tight little shake of her head. "He doesn't date," she said. "I'm never going to get him to ask me out." As if she even wanted to. Cole had come to town two years ago when Chief Rasband retired. He was devilishly handsome, sure. A double hit to the heart with that uniform and that cowboy hat, definitely.

And Berlin would not be the first female to try to charm the man since he'd come to town. As she watched a bubbly blonde named Tiffany approach and flirt with the man, she realized she wouldn't even be the first woman to attempt to get his attention *tonight*.

"Go on," Caitlyn hissed and gave her another push.

Berlin was going to fail miserably, but a deal was a deal.

Help me, she prayed with every step toward the carnival games. *Give me the right words. Make him like brunettes with ashy black hair. Just get me through this deal.*

After all, if she lost, her friends had dreamed up a terrible consequence for her, and she would not give them the satisfaction of setting her up on a dozen blind dates.

CHAPTER 2

Cole dismissed the giggly blonde, much to his men's cajoling. He didn't so much as crack a smile. He'd agreed to come to this summer fair in uniform though he wasn't on duty. But he had never agreed to dealing with women wearing too little clothing and too much perfume.

"Come on, boss," one of his men, Jordan, said. "She was cute."

"And about twenty years younger than me," Cole growled, scanning the crowd. His eyes missed nothing, though he felt like he was wearing a mask. After all, he was a public figure, and the people of Brush Creek were constantly judging him.

He thought he'd done a decent job in the twenty-four months since he'd arrived in town. His public reviews were good—high, even—and he did loathe going home to only Sarge and Honor, as awesome as his German shepherds were.

In fact, some nights, he just slept in his office, and some of the men had started calling it his lair.

"So an older woman," Jordan said, bent on getting Cole a date.

"I'm fine," he said, though his mother's words streamed through his mind on a constant loop.

Are you dating anyone?

No? Why not?

Someone needs to get married and give me some grandbabies.

As if Cole was the only Fairbanks man who hadn't tied the knot yet. He sat right in the middle of five boys, and none of his brothers had gotten married yet. As far as he knew, only Mathias even had a girlfriend at the moment. So why his mother was badgering him was a mystery to Cole.

Not really, he told himself as he and the two officers he walked with moved toward the food stands. He'd put her off for a decade by saying he wasn't interested in starting a relationship with a woman when he wasn't settled. He hadn't really bounced around, but he did go wherever the best opportunity for advancement existed.

He'd finally settled at the top, as Chief of Police, and his mother knew it. And yet, Cole still hadn't been out with a woman in Brush Creek. He hadn't really been looking, because while he'd worked, slaved, gone to school and attended trainings for years to get where he was, he hadn't realized how *busy* the Chief would be.

"All right, Chief," Mason said. The lieutenant stepped in front of him. "Let's make a bet. Ten dates. You need to go on ten dates, or...." He exchanged a glance with Jordan, whose dark eyes glittered under the lights along the Ferris wheel.

"Ten dates?" Cole glared at his captain and then the lieutenant. "With the same woman?"

"Could be ten different women." Mason looked at Jordan, who shrugged. "Sure, ten different women. But it can't take forever."

"Three months. The summer." Jordan nodded to a couple of ladies walking by, and their twittering made Cole want to run for the hills. Why did women think that sound made them more attractive? But apparently, to men like Jordan, it did, because he turned around and watched them walk the other direction, his gaze aglow.

"You actually are on duty." Cole grabbed Jordan's collar and pulled him around so he was walking forward.

Jordan chuckled and straightened his uniform. "You're such a beast."

"So three months," Mason said, falling back in line beside Cole and ignoring the glare Cole sent his way. "Ten dates. Or...or what?"

"Or he gives us his bonus check this year," Jordan said, a measure of glee in his voice that annoyed Cole from the ground up.

"I'm not giving you my bonus check."

"You buy the whole department dinner," Mason suggested.

"*And* you can't sleep in your office until the ten dates are done," Jordan added.

"Dinner," Cole mused. The police department in Brush Creek wasn't that big, but it would still be a few hundred dollars to feed them all. "Ten dates." Honestly, he'd rather buy the department dinner and be done with it.

"Doesn't have to be the same woman," Mason reminded him. "Just...come *on*. Women are obviously interested in you. Why are you so opposed to going out with one of them?"

"Beast," Jordan whispered but it was still definitely loud enough for Cole to hear above the noise of the fair.

"It's...." Cole didn't mind being friendly with his guys. But he wasn't *friends* with them. He didn't have them over for weekend barbecues, and he didn't discuss his personal life with them. Period. The end.

So he didn't want to tell them that no one in Brush Creek had caught his eye. Of course, he spent a lot of time behind brick walls at the station, and the only people coming in and out of there worked in the building or were being booked into jail. Neither of those presented viable options for finding a date. And maybe he liked his bachelor status. Had anyone ever thought of that? Maybe he acted a bit beastly to preserve his sanity, keep his heart in one piece, and enjoy the calmness of this town where he'd landed.

"Look," Jordan said. "Just *try* with the next woman who comes over."

"What makes you think another woman will come over?" Cole cast Jordan a sideways glance.

He nodded to Cole's right. "Because she's comin' right now."

Cole swung his attention in the direction of Jordan's gaze to find a beautiful brunette walking across the grass. She had obviously been dressed up nice, and she had those ridiculous eyelashes all the girls were wearing now. But somehow...somehow the cop in him saw past the façade to the woman underneath.

None of it belonged to her. The clothes, the makeup, the tiny purse she clutched like it was her very key to surviving. As she stopped in a halo of orange light, Cole realized even the hair was fake. No one naturally had hair that color.

But he liked it, and a slow smile worked its way through his body until it touched his mouth. The woman was younger than him too, but most available females were. As he pushed closer and closer to forty, that couldn't be helped.

"Can I help you?" Mason asked, a snicker not far behind the question. For some reason, Cole wanted to punch the lieutenant so this beautiful woman wouldn't feel self-conscious.

Her gaze settled on Mason and she leaned in closer to say something to him. He grinned and said, "Oh, I see one of those teenagers we were looking for earlier. Jordan, let's go talk to them."

They both practically ran out of there like someone had set fire to their heels, leaving Cole alone with the only woman who'd sparked his interested in the past decade.

"Hey." She ran the tip of her tongue between her lips, a classic sign of nerves. That, plus the way she choked her purse, was a dead giveaway. "So listen, I sort of made a deal with my friends, and all I need you to do is agree to go out with me." She held up her hands and shook them like she meant him no harm. "We don't actually have to go out. I mean, I know you don't date, and well, the deal was they could pick, and they picked you, and I really don't want—"

She stopped talking when he raised his hand, an indication for her to do so. "You know I don't date?"

"No, sir." She pressed her eyes closed and shook her heard. "Or, yes, sir. Yes, I know you don't date." She drew in a deep breath. "Sir."

Oh, how he hated the word *sir* when it came out of her mouth. In many other situations, he loved the respect he commanded. But not this time. Not with her.

"What's your name?"

"Berlin Fuller."

He nodded and scanned the area behind her, finding the peanut gallery stationed over by the lemonade stand. "Are those your friends?" He waved to them, putting a great, big smile on his face.

Berlin half-turned back to them and then faced him with the most miserable look on her face, her gaze on the ground. "I wasn't supposed to tell you about the deal."

"Deal? What deal?"

Her eyes—the brightest, bluest eyes he'd ever seen, and probably the only real thing about this Berlin Fuller —latched onto his. Everything at the summer fair fell away. Cole had never been distracted like this before, on duty or off. But Berlin glowed like a heavenly being, and a craving to know more about her pulled through him in a way he didn't understand. Had never felt before.

Not only was he going to ask her out, Cole actually *wanted* to see her again. *Ten times?* he wondered.

He wasn't sure on the last part, but if there was one thing seventeen years in police work had taught him, it was to be patient. Take one step at a time. Learn one fact, and then learn the next.

So he didn't need to know if he could endure ten dates with Berlin. He'd start with one and see how things went. And if he didn't have to buy his department a steak dinner, well, that was just an added side benefit.

So Sunday afternoon? Cole stared at the text, imagining what Berlin would look like without all the makeup. Sundays were always more casual for Cole, and he hoped Berlin would leave the heeled boots and mini skirts at home if he took her out in the afternoon.

He sent the text, glad he'd come away from the fair with a woman's phone number this year. The previous two years, he'd left with a massive headache and a general disdain for teenagers.

He'd walked around with Berlin for twenty or thirty minutes before she gave him her number and said to text her his first available time. He'd told her he was busy, and she'd said she worked nine to five at a company in town.

Sarge lifted his big head when Cole's phone buzzed, and Cole scrubbed the German shepherd's head while he picked up his device. "It's Berlin." He smiled and read the message.

Sunday afternoon is great. Two o'clock?

Two's great.

Will we be eating?

I can always eat, he typed. You?

I'll eat a late breakfast and call that lunch.

Cole confirmed, wondering what in the world he was doing. Was this how dating worked now? Meeting, talking for a few minutes, exchanging numbers, and then texting.

Apparently so, as she continued messaging him for the next hour, continuing their conversation from the park with questions like *How many siblings do you have?* and *Where are you from?*

Basic get-to-know-you stuff. All the stuff Cole normally despised, another reason he hadn't really tried to find a girlfriend or a wife. It was so much *work* getting to know someone, and honestly, Cole had his plate full when it came to things that took work.

But as a picture of a cute gray and white dog came through his text stream, he decided this phone dating wasn't so hard.

My Lhasa Apso, Brownie. Do you have pets?

Cole grinned at the fact that Berlin was a fellow dog-lover. She'd said he didn't even have to go out with her, but as he sent pictures of Honor and then Sarge, and she sent over a brown and white Lhasa Apso named Cocoa, Cole found he couldn't wait until Sunday at two o'clock.

Until she asked if where they'd be going for "lunch" had any vegetarian options.

He rolled his eyes and groaned. He didn't want Berlin to be a vegetarian when he loved every kind of meat this great planet had to offer.

He skipped the question and asked if she wanted to just grab something from the bakery instead.

The bakery's closed on Sundays, came her reply. *And I can't meet until after church anyway.*

Cole put his phone down at that point, realizing how late it was and how the conversation had taken a turn he didn't like. So he and Berlin liked dogs. He found her beautiful. Didn't mean they were a match, especially if she liked everything he didn't.

A twinge of guilt pulled through him that his phone buzzed a few more times and he didn't answer. But now he had that headache he'd experienced the last couple of years, and he didn't want to say something *beastly* he couldn't take back.

CHAPTER 3

Berlin didn't hear from Cole again until one-thirty on Sunday. She'd texted him several times, and it was like he'd just shut off. A thread of trepidation pulled through her as she brushed out her hair after church.

Wren had invited her to lunch, and Berlin had said she wasn't feeling up to it. She loved her oldest sister Wren, who had the cutest little girl named Etta. She and Tate were expecting again, as were two other women in the Fuller family.

Cora and Brennan lived in California, and he'd finished his landscape architecture degree two months ago. Cora worked as a hotshot, but she'd be taking a leave of absence once their baby came in November.

Dawn also had a baby bump these days, due in December just before the holidays. Out of all her sisters, Berlin had thought at least she'd never have to worry about Dawn living up to their mother's standards. She'd been telling everyone for years that she didn't want to be a mother. Ironic, considering she became one the moment she married McDermott, five years ago.

Berlin noticed she was making a face, and she derailed the thoughts about her family members. Fabi and Jazzy had only been married for a couple of years, but Berlin expected them to announce pregnancies any day now.

"And I can't even get a date." She turned away from her reflection, hating how light her eyebrows were. Starlee had asked her if she should dye them too, but Berlin had panicked and said no. She liked the dark-haired look, but it felt...odd with the eyebrows. Like something wasn't quite right.

She stared at her phone, at Cole's message that said, Am I picking you up? and wondered if she should just blow him off. She thought of those broad shoulders filling out his police uniform. That sexy cowboy hat. The way he'd devoured her within seconds of looking at her. The man was powerful, intimidating, and absolutely made her heart race with excitement. And if there was something Berlin needed in her life, it was an adventure.

"Sure, you can pick me up," she said aloud to her two small dogs as she typed the words into her texting app. She added her address and sent the message.

Great. See you soon. Cole didn't seem like a man of many words, and Berlin's chest squeezed. What in the world would they talk about? He'd seemed okay with the topics they'd been texting about on Friday night—work, dogs, and their families. She'd been surprised that he didn't know much about hers, but he was a transplant to Brush Creek, and her father didn't serve on the City Council anymore.

In fact, her parents were getting older, and her dad had already started to draw up paperwork to turn the company over to Milt. As Berlin worked as the business's accountant, she was privy to all kinds of insider information the other siblings weren't. Sometimes she liked that, because as the youngest, she was rarely included in important family decisions. And sometimes she didn't need to know the minutia of the company.

The minutes slipped by while she thought about the week's work ahead of her, and before she knew it, Cole had arrived at her house. She knew it was Cole, because he rapped authoritatively three times *and* called her name, as if he needed to announce his presence so she'd open the door.

She smoothed her hands down her jeans, hoping it wouldn't be too hot for them wherever Cole was taking her. But she didn't feel the need to dress up to the nines for an afternoon date, especially when he'd already seen her trying too hard at the summer fair.

So jeans, sandals, and a flowery top would have to do. She opened the door to find him wearing a delicious pair of dark wash jeans too. His polo shirt was the color of tangerines, and had white and black stripes going across it, only accentuating the width of his chest and the bulge of his biceps.

Berlin's mouth turned dry, making swallowing—and speaking—very difficult.

His close-cropped hair broadcasted his police status, and he hadn't shaved that day, giving him a rough-around-the-edges sexiness Berlin had no defense against. She wanted to reach out and touch his scruff, cradle his face as she brought it closer to hers, inhale the summery, citrusy, woodsy scent of his skin.

"You look nice," he said, his smile revealing a beautiful set of white teeth. "Are you ready?" He looked over her shoulder and into her house. "Ah, there are the pups." He bent down like she had no affect on him whatsoever and started rubbing Brownie and Cocoa. The dogs seemed to wear smiles as his big hands touched them, and Berlin couldn't blame them one bit.

"I'm ready," she managed to push past the lump in her throat. This was such a bad idea. He'd probably only agreed to go out with her out of pity, and she added, "You don't have to do this, you know. I just needed to get a date, and I got one."

He straightened, his dark gray eyes reminding her of deep, dangerous storm clouds as they rolled over the horizon and threatened to dump rain on the town. "I want to go out with you." He spoke without a rasp or a hitch in his voice. "And it wasn't easy finding something to do on Sunday, let me tell you. It's like this town shuts down."

Berlin shouldered her purse and stepped out onto the porch with him, leaving her dogs inside. They had a doggy door in the back that let them out into the yard, and she'd already refilled their food and water.

"So what are we doing?" she asked. "Eating isn't necessary."

He guided her down her own steps with slight pressure on the small of her back. The touch was light, casual, but it sent fireworks through Berlin's muscles and she could barely walk. Was she imagining this electricity between them? She cast a glance over her shoulder to Cole, who seemed calm, cool, collected. Utterly nonplussed.

He smiled at her again. "Eating is always necessary. In fact, I don't think we can call this a date if there's no eating."

Somehow her lips curved upward too, and she slid into his muscle car easily. "This is your police vehicle?" she asked when he positioned his tall frame behind the wheel. She'd never seen so many switches and buttons and screens before.

"That's right." He put the car in gear and it didn't take long for her to figure out they were leaving Brush Creek. "So I thought we'd try this place I found in Beaverton a while back. The Crepe Factory?" He cut a glance at her out of the side of his eye, but mostly focused on the road with both hands on the wheel.

"Sure, sounds great." Berlin infused her voice with as much positivity as she could. But she'd been to The Crepe Factory, and it wasn't that great. Nothing coming from a factory could be, in her opinion, but she pressed that opinion behind closed lips.

The drive happened in ten minutes, and Cole didn't say a word. Berlin had never felt so awkward, and she wondered why Caitlyn and Scott had thought this man, handsome and powerful as he was, was perfect for her. Even Gray had made her feel at ease in his presence, and he'd had just as much experience as Cole.

He parked and said, "I thought this would work since you don't eat meat."

"I eat meat," she said.

He turned toward her, his eyebrows up. "Really? You asked if there would be vegetarian options. I guess I just assumed."

Feeling brave and bold and a little out of control, Berlin said, "Well, that's your first mistake." She flashed him the flirtiest smile she could, her spirits dampened when he simply continued to stare at her. A sigh passed through her body and she reached for the door handle. This was going to be the shortest date in her pathetic history, and then she'd have to pray she never ran into the Chief of Police again.

She managed to make small talk while they waited for their order. The crepes were not any better this time than the last time she'd been here with Caitlyn, but Cole paid, and then they got back in the car.

Sure enough, he arrived back in her driveway before an hour had passed. Her chest tightened, and she couldn't get any words out. Not that she wanted to ask to see him again; she didn't think he'd perpetuate the relationship either.

He did play the perfect gentleman and get out, open her door, and walk her to the porch. "Okay," he said. "Thanks for coming with me."

She nodded, her emotions so close to the surface she didn't dare vocalize anything.

"I'll talk to you later?" He made it sound like a question, but he didn't wait for her to answer. He gave a military nod like what he'd said was now law and he strode back to his cruiser.

She ducked behind the safety of her front door and told herself not to rush to the bedroom window so she could watch him drive out of her life. She did it anyway, Brownie putting his front paws up on the wall as if he could stretch tall enough to see the police car brake at the corner and then turn left and disappear.

"Worst date ever," she muttered as she sank down to the ground and pulled out her phone to text Caitlyn.

MONDAY MORNING, Berlin arrived at the offices of A Jack of All Trades an hour before she needed to be there. Wren wouldn't be in for at least another two hours, and that was just fine with Berlin. She needed some time to get settled for the week, and she did *not* want to talk about her date with Cole.

Her phone rang before twenty minutes had gone by, and

Berlin swiped on the call though she didn't know who it was. It was a local Brush Creek number, so it could be anyone.

"Berlin Fuller," she said, thinking she could be authoritative and commanding if she had to be. Her job simply didn't demand that she needed to be.

"Berlin, glad I got you. I was worried it would be too early."

She cocked her head, trying to figure out who she was talking to. They obviously knew her, but she couldn't place the voice. "Not too early," she said, buying herself some time to make the connection.

"It's Paul Shafer from the City Controller's office. I'm wondering if you have a few minutes this morning to meet with me."

Berlin stopped trying to organize her paperwork for the day. "Today?"

"The City Council has approved a budget to do an independent audit of the police department."

She sat heavily in her chair. "Oh-kay."

"Come on over to my office, and I'll give you all the details." He didn't wait for her to confirm, didn't set up a time, nothing. He just hung up, leaving Berlin to stare at her phone and wonder why every man thought what he said would simply be followed.

Her stomach writhed, and her blood heated. But she stood, collected her briefcase, and headed for the door. Though no one ever came to see her in the office, she still wore professional clothes. *Dress the part.* She believed in that, and today, her navy skirt suit would come in quite handy as she crossed the street and went down a block to the city offices.

Paul had an office on the third floor, and she knocked when she arrived. Without waiting for him to invite her in, she strode forward and shook his hand. "Morning, Paul." She perched on the edge of the straight-backed chair available across from him. "Tell me about this audit."

"Wow, look at you." He leaned back in his chair and surveyed her, stalling on her ridiculous dark hair and light eyebrows. He blinked, which apparently allowed him to speak again. "You have a master's degree in accounting?"

"I do." She'd taken most of her classes online, right here in Brush Creek while she did the bookkeeping for the family business. She'd left town for a couple of years to finish in Colorado Springs, on-site, and then she'd promptly come back. She liked things that lined up, and numbers that added up, and life to be simple and uncomplicated.

"The City Council would like to hire you to do the financial audit."

"Don't they have their own internal auditor?" she asked.

"They do, but it's been proposed and accepted that there be an independent audit, done by someone with no interest in the outcomes. We just need someone to do the job and give us the report." He tilted his head and steepled his fingers. "Can you do that?"

"Of course." She'd participated in an audit of a huge insurance firm while in her last year of college. It had been nightmarish work, though, and she didn't want to do another audit, ever. Especially of her hometown police department. "Perhaps, though—"

"Great." Paul leaned forward and tossed a card on his desk. "There's Chief Fairbanks's personal line. Call his secretary and set up an appointment to see him. He should be able to help you with everything you need."

Berlin blinked, her muscles, bones, and blood turning numb. "Chief Fairbanks," she repeated. He could most certainly *not* help her with everything she needed, as evidenced by yesterday's disastrous afternoon.

Fifty-four minutes, her brain whispered. And twenty of those had been spent driving. She picked up the card and slipped it into her hollow briefcase. "How long do I have?"

"Ninety days," he said. "And we'd like you to come to all the City Council meetings between now and then for updates."

"Every week?" Berlin couldn't keep the horror out of her voice. She'd lived through her father being on the Council, and sometimes the Tuesday night meetings went until midnight. Everything in her rebelled at the idea of attending the City Council meetings, because not only did she crave her free time in the evenings, but she knew the Chief of Police also went.

Auditing the police department and going to Council meetings was not the way to avoid seeing him.

But Paul stood, the meeting clearly over, and said, "As often as you can. Obviously not tomorrow, as you'll have just started. I'll report that you've taken the assignment. There's a budget and all the paperwork for you to get paid. Let's see...." He rummaged around on his desk for a moment, finally coming up with a manila folder. "Here you go. Let me know if you have any questions."

He sat down and picked up the phone, her cue to take the folder and go. Back in the privacy and safety of her own office, she pulled out the papers and examined them. The budget for her to complete the audit was huge —easily twice her yearly salary here at A Jack of All Trades.

A smile slipped across her face. Maybe this much money was worth having to face the surly Chief of Police a few more times. How hard could it be? She probably wouldn't even have to talk to him. Surely he had a secretary, and Berlin could likely get what she needed for the audit from that person.

Still, she put off calling over to the police department for a couple of days. Mostly because she really did have a ton of paperwork and reports to finish for her own business, but partly because she held a blip of fear at dialing the Chief's personal number and demanding all their financial documents for the past five years.

Thursday afternoon, Wren poked her head into

Berlin's office and said, "I'm taking off early. See you tomorrow."

With the office quiet, and Berlin mostly caught up on the quarterly reports, she summoned the courage she needed to make the phone call.

"Chief Fairbanks," Cole barked into the line after only one ring.

"Oh." Berlin had been expecting the secretary to answer, and she had no idea what to say now.

A squeak came through the line, like he'd leaned back in his desk chair and it was protesting. "Can I help you?" He'd asked her the same thing at the summer fair, almost a week ago.

"It's Berlin," she said, making her voice as brusque as his. "Berlin Fuller? I'm performing the independent audit of your department, and I'm wondering what your schedule looks like? I need to meet with you."

Chapter 4

Cole's mood went from sour to downright dangerous with Berlin's words. *I need to meet with you.*

So he hadn't asked her out again. Hadn't called. Or texted. The date had been awful, if he was being honest with himself. He felt something move through his blood when he looked at Berlin, but he wasn't sure what it was. Perhaps simple attraction.

He'd appreciated her casual attire on Sunday, and she'd carried the conversation. Truth was, Cole didn't know how to date. Didn't know how to make a woman feel at ease. He'd spent his whole life learning how to get people to tell him the truth, and that usually made people squirm a bit.

"Are you there?" she asked. "Did I lose you?" Even her voice sent shockwaves through him.

"I'm here," he said. "I'm looking at my schedule." He

clicked on his computer so he wouldn't be a liar and pulled up his calendar.

"You don't have a secretary that manages things for you?" she asked.

Of course he did. But Lesli was on vacation this week and most of next, and he could look at a calendar as well as she could anyway. He grunted, which could've meant yes or no. "I have some time tomorrow morning, first thing, or next Tuesday right after lunch."

Berlin exhaled like neither of those times would work. He could juggle a few things, move a meeting if he had to. But he waited for her to speak. She'd told him she was the accountant for her family's business, and while he knew the City Council would be performing an independent audit of the department's finances, he'd had no idea who they'd hire to do it. Guess he knew now.

"Might as well get it over with," she said. "What time tomorrow morning?"

He scowled though she wasn't in the room and couldn't see him. *Might as well get it over with.* Like seeing him was such a chore. He supposed he hadn't been super nice or charming on Sunday, but he couldn't fix it now.

"I come in at seven-thirty," he said. "I have another appointment at nine-thirty. So those two hours are yours, if you want them."

"Do you think we'll need two hours?"

"How would I know?" Cole took a deep breath and schooled his voice into civility. "I'm at your mercy, Miss

Fuller. I've never been through a department audit. I'll leave it up to you to decide how long we need to meet."

A healthy pause came through the line, and then she said. "I'll see you at seven-thirty. Do you drink coffee?"

"Yes," he said, wondering what that had to do with anything.

"What about doughnuts? Do you eat those?"

"Is this a bad cop joke?" He narrowed his eyes at his closed door, wishing he'd been nicer, better, something during their date. In a town the size of Brush Creek, he should've known he'd have to see her again.

She laughed, the sound magical and making his bad mood dry up instantly. "No, Chief. I'm wondering if I can bring coffee and pastries in the morning to, uh, make the meeting go smoother." She gave another low laugh. "You seem like a black coffee kind of guy, who...probably gets up at five to work out. Run ten miles or something. So maybe a simple croissant?"

"Black coffee is fine," he said. He had his own supply of specialty sugars and fancy creams, but she didn't need to know that. He could doctor up the coffee in the building's kitchen while she looked through some boring paperwork. "And I'll take one of those bear claws from Erin's."

"Oh, a bear claw. Chocolate or cinnamon? Wait, let me guess."

If Cole didn't know better—if he hadn't completely blundered their date a few days ago—he'd have said Berlin was flirting with him.

"Chocolate," they said together, and that finally elicited a chuckle from Cole. "See you tomorrow, Miss Fuller."

"Oh, come on, Chief," she said. "You can call me Berlin."

"Then you can call me Cole." Did he have another chance with her? He hadn't gone out with anyone else this week, as Jordan and Mason liked to remind him each morning when they popped their heads in to say "Eighty-five days left, Chief. One date," the countdown apparently switching between the two of them.

"See you tomorrow...Cole." Berlin hung up, and Cole wondered if a business meeting where someone brought coffee and doughnuts for the other could be considered a date.

WHEN COLE PULLED up to the station at seven twenty-five the next morning, Berlin was already there, standing beside her car. A brown pastry box sat on the top, as did a single to-go cup of coffee. She held hers in her hand, sipping it as she leaned against her car and watched him.

She wore a pair of black slacks, black heels, and a blouse the color of lemons. It made her skin seem darker than it was, and her hair shone like black gold under the morning sunlight. So Cole found her beautiful. Exotic, almost, like he'd never seen anyone like her before.

The spark that had first attracted him to her flared to life again, and he took an extra moment pretending to gather what he needed from the car to pray for strength. While he hadn't darkened the doorway of a church in several years, his mama had taught him to believe in God and love the Lord. So if he threw up a few prayers here and there, Cole at least felt like he wasn't too bad of a son.

He finally got out of the car and approached her. She looked at her phone, her eyes flitting right past his. "Seven twenty-seven. Right on time."

"You're early." He accepted the coffee cup she handed him, but he didn't take a sip. Her keen gaze didn't miss a single thing and she nodded toward the pastry box. He collected it and she bent to retrieve her briefcase, which she'd set at her feet.

"I don't like to be late," she said. "And I really dislike it when others are late."

"Me too." He seized onto this tidbit of information, so glad they had something else in common. It seemed like everything they'd talked about was surface stuff or only proved to him how opposite they were. And while opposites definitely attracted, he didn't want to spend his life seeking out restaurants with vegetarian options.

Don't be a beast. Mason's words from last night, when Cole had told him Berlin was coming in the morning for the audit, haunted him. It wasn't like Cole liked appraising every person who approached him, every situation presented to him. It was simply what he'd spent his life doing.

He opened the door for her and waited for Berlin to pass him. He caught a whiff of her perfume, getting a nose full of flowers and sugar. She'd obviously already consumed a doughnut, and he wondered how long she'd been waiting in the parking lot.

He liked the way she carried herself with confidence, her shoulders square and her head held high. She'd piled her hair on top of her head in some sort of up-do that could've been worn to prom. Cole wondered how old she was. He obviously knew she was younger than him, but the difference was important.

"How old are you?" he blurted.

She slowed and stopped, turned and quirked one eyebrow at him. "Excuse me?" Her grip tightened on her briefcase, and Cole wasn't sure if he was glad he noticed every little detail or not.

"I'm sorry. Never mind." He could just look her up in the system. She had a driver's license. She turned and kept walking toward his corner office, almost like she'd been there before.

He mentally kicked himself and told himself to talk softer. Ask more roundabout questions. Or none at all. This wasn't a date, and if the independent auditor were anyone but Berlin Fuller, he'd have left the cases of files on the front step and told the guy to stop by and pick them up.

Sighing, he eased himself into the room with her, coaching himself to be nice. *Be nice. Be nice.*

"Have a seat." He gestured to the two chairs in front of his desk. "Please," he added as an afterthought.

Berlin flashed him a tight smile and sat, pulling out a sheet of paper from her briefcase. "Okay." She exhaled slowly, like air leaking from a balloon. "I'm not here to audit internal investigations, police shootings, in-custody deaths, or complaints." She glanced up. "I assume you have an in-house auditor for those things?"

Cole shifted in his seat. "It's on my to-do list." He'd only been in this job for a couple of years, and it was a small town. An in-house auditor required money, and budget approval, and Cole hadn't gotten to it yet.

"Oh, well, it's not required." Berlin spoke with an air of nonchalance, though it was clear she thought he should have an in-house auditor for those things. It wasn't a bad idea, though he hadn't experienced any police shootings or in-custody deaths since he'd been here. Brush Creek PD hadn't in the last eight years, in fact. So he'd had a hard time adding it to the department budget.

"I'm just here for the financials," she said. "So I need ledgers for revenue and expenses, payroll accounts, including all overtime reports, and grant activity, billing procedures, and charity fund accounting." She met his eye. "There's more." She handed him the paper, and he took it without taking his eyes off of her.

Could she feel that current between them? Or was the room just too small?

Berlin cleared her throat and shifted on the seat, crossing her legs and looking straight into his eyes again. "I'm sure you know what I need."

"Indeed I do." It wasn't his first audit, though it was the first where he sat at the helm of the whole department. Even though he'd only been here for a couple of years, it would still be his name at the top of the report when it was published.

He cocked his head at her. "Tell me I'm not crazy."

"Pardon?" She folded her arms across her chest, and Cole's attraction to her doubled.

He leaned forward, the air practically crackling between them. "Let's try again," he said. "And I'll not be in such a...bad mood."

"Try what again, exactly?"

So she was going to make him say it. "Dating. Me and you. What's your schedule like tonight?"

Her eyes widened, and she leaned toward him again. "You're kind of intimidating. Did you know that?"

"I've heard that before," he said coolly. "But I swear I don't mean to come off that way. It's just...I'm just...."

"Tall," she said. "Dark." She didn't blink, and her mouth barely moved when she added, "Handsome," to the list.

So he wasn't imagining things. He hadn't truly thought he was, but it was nice to know. As a cop, he was trained to take what he believed and forget about it. Search for the truth instead.

He hated the wide desk between them. "Would you like to go to dinner tonight?" He gave her the smile his last crush had told him made her entire chest melt. Cole couldn't help it if he had a dazzling smile. He had to have something to offset his prickly personality.

Berlin's fingers flitted around her throat and a beautiful blush climbed into her face. "Dinner would be fine. But I don't like that crepe place."

"It was pretty bad, wasn't it?" He chuckled. "Mine wasn't even cooked all the way and it only had about three strawberries inside."

She laughed, the sound getting trapped up in the corners. Cole basked in it, his heart softening toward this woman.

When she quieted, he said, "So tell me where to go. I want the food to be good, and the atmosphere to be awesome, and I'll be on my best behavior."

"Teddy's?" she suggested. "It's this great place on the highway up by Maple Mountain. They have live music on the weekends and great food." Her eyes positively sparkled when she said, "Lots of red meat."

Cole laughed this time and he stood. "Are you going to eat the meat?"

"I get the pulled pork sandwich there," she said, looking up at him. "But I'm willing to branch out."

It felt like they weren't talking about the menu anymore, and Cole cleared his throat. "Let me get you the files you need for the audit. If we don't get started on it, we might not make it to dinner tonight."

A look of panic crossed Berlin's beautiful face. "That much stuff, huh?"

"It's been five years since this department has had a financial audit," he said. "I hope they gave you a decent chunk of time to do this. Don't you have a full-time job already?"

"Yeah." She sighed and scraped a few errant strands of hair off the side of her face. "They gave me ninety days."

Cole whistled. "That's gonna be a tight race." He stepped over to the door and opened it. "I'll help you with the boxes."

CHAPTER 5

Berlin immensely enjoyed watching Cole bend and flex and lift box after box. She was not overly excited about the number of them. They took up the entire backseat of her sedan, the whole trunk, and he stacked three in the front passenger seat too.

Ninety days was definitely not long enough to get this audit completed, and she'd need to talk to the City Controller about getting more time. Paul hadn't seemed like he was willing to accept any compromise from her, but she'd insist based on her full-time employment outside the scope of this audit.

"So how much to hire your muscles for an hour?" She gripped her keys until the jagged edges dug into her skin.

"I'm sorry, what?"

"How am I going to get all these boxes into my

office?" She'd carried out two and then let Cole use his strength to get the job done.

He leaned against his cruiser, and he looked so darn good doing it, Berlin's heart started hammering out of control. "I'll follow you over."

"Do you know where my office is?"

"No idea."

"We're right behind the movie theater." She opened the driver's side door. "Just a couple of blocks down."

"All right then." He got in his car, and Berlin led the way to the nondescript office building.

When he pulled up beside her and got out, he said, "I live right there." He pointed to the house across the street and kitty-corner to the office building. It was in a row of houses that all looked similar with tan stucco and white trim. A huge, hulking black SUV sat in the driveway. As if the scruff wasn't manly enough. Or the shoulders as wide as the Mississippi. Or the twinkling gray eyes. And the police badge.

Berlin wasn't sure how she was supposed to work twelve hours a day this summer when she knew Cole was a two-minute walk away. Even the police station wasn't that far from her office.

"Nice house," she said, wondering if the SUV was his. Maybe he had a roommate. A brother living with him. Something.

"Thanks."

"You do the yard work and everything yourself?"

"No, I hire it out."

Of course he did. Berlin wasn't sure of all of Cole's responsibilities, but they were surely numerous and never finished. "Who do you use?"

"A Jack of All Trades."

Berlin ducked her head. He had no idea who she really was. "That's my family's company."

He swung his attention toward her. "It is?"

"Yeah. Is it Milt or Pat that comes?"

"Milt."

Berlin popped the trunk and indicated the boxes. "My dad's retiring soon, so Milt will be taking over. I'm glad you like our services."

Cole joined her at the trunk. "Oh, I like them." But he wasn't looking at the yard anymore.

Berlin half snorted and half scoffed before she nudged him with her elbow. "Let's get these inside. I have about twenty hours of work to do today and only ten to do it in."

"So should I pick you up here?" He lifted two boxes into his arms effortlessly, and Berlin simply watched as his muscles rippled.

"No." She shook her head adamantly. "I'll go home and slip into something a little more date-like."

"I liked the jeans on Sunday," he said.

"Something casual, then?" she asked, following him to the building and holding open the door for him. "For a Friday night date?"

"I don't care what you wear," he said, pausing to gaze

down into her face. "Just don't cover up that pretty face with too much makeup."

A shock moved through Berlin, but part of her really liked that Cole said what he thought. Maybe he was a little too blunt sometimes. Maybe he couldn't hide how he was feeling when he should've. Maybe he was a bit on the ornery side. But he was cute, and Berlin couldn't deny the supreme attraction she felt for him.

Besides, he's just said that she had a pretty face. Oh, Cole Fairbanks had a soft side, she decided as he unloaded the twenty-one boxes of financial documents. She just needed to get him to invite her to see it.

———

BERLIN DIDN'T FEEL like jeans were appropriate for a Friday night date. Especially at Teddy's, which was a happening place even in the middle of the week. Friday night, the restaurant would be slammed, and she texted Cole in a panic about the wait time.

I'll get a reservation, he sent back. Berlin wanted to argue that they didn't take reservations and maybe they should go somewhere else. But when he'd said he wanted to go somewhere with great food and a lively atmosphere, the only place Berlin could settle on was Teddy's. Sure, there were great places right in Brush Creek, but she was hoping Cole's physical skills extended to dancing.

Berlin loved dancing to live music, and six o'clock came both faster and slower than she liked. This time, when Cole knocked on the door, it didn't sound like he was trying to knock it into the next county.

When she opened the door, he stood back a few feet, his hands tucked in his jeans pockets. The man made denim look amazing, and tonight, he wore a purple and blue checkered shirt that was slightly too tight in the biceps.

And that black cowboy hat was so sinful Berlin felt like she'd need to visit the pastor later to make sure she was still on good ground with the Lord.

She leaned in the doorway and smiled. "All you need is a belt buckle and you'd be a real cowboy."

He chuckled, the sound drawing her dogs out onto the porch, where he bent down and scratched them like he had last time. At least he got along with them, because Berlin and her pups came as a package deal.

"Who takes care of your dogs all day?" she asked.

"Oh, they're at the station half of the time." He straightened and reached his hand toward her as if he wanted to hold hands with her. She looked at his fingers and as if her hand had a mind of its own, she locked her grip with his.

Everything inside her tripped, and her heart stalled for one long, delicious beat while he squeezed her fingers. "See? Already better than last time."

She laughed, because that was all she could do. "That was a pretty horrible date, wasn't it?"

He shrugged and shooed the dogs back inside before

drawing her front door closed. "I've had worse, if you can believe it."

"No." Berlin shook her head and wrapped her other hand around hers and Cole's. "I don't believe that."

"Well, it's true." He drew her toward the passenger side of his police vehicle. "I'm not…I don't date a lot."

"You don't say." Berlin gazed up at him, feeling like someone had dumped sparkles in her blood. "Why is that, by the way?"

His gaze softened the teensiest bit as he reached behind her to open the door. "It took a lot of long hours, and special courses, and tactical training to get this job."

Berlin ducked into the car, wondering why he took his city vehicle when he had that SUV. He got behind the wheel as she realized the interior smelled like oranges today when it hadn't on Sunday.

"Have you always wanted to be a cop?" she asked.

"Yes."

"The Chief."

"Yes." He didn't bark the answers today like he had last time, but he didn't ask her any questions.

"How old are you?" she asked as he pulled onto the highway that led north to Maple Mountain.

"Oh, so you can ask me, but I can't ask you?"

"It's rude to ask a woman her age," Berlin said, adding a light laugh—decidedly not a giggle—to her statement. Caitlyn had told her she'd heard through the grapevine that the Chief did not like giggling women.

Berlin didn't like them much herself, but there was something about Cole that made her giddy—and giggly.

"If I tell you, will you tell me?"

"Sure."

His jaw twitched once. "I'm thirty-seven."

Only ten years older than her. No one could understand the relief that cascaded through her. Gray had been fifteen years older, and everyone had had a problem with it.

"Ever been married?" she asked.

"No."

"And you already said you don't date much."

"I've moved a lot too," he said. "So that was another reason I didn't get serious with anyone."

"But you're in Brush Creek to stay, right?" Berlin didn't need to start something with him if he'd only be here for a few months.

"Don't worry about that."

"That's not a yes or a no."

He looked at her, abandoning his careful study of the road in front of him though he kept his hands at ten and two on the wheel. "I'm in town to stay," he said. "As long as they'll have me."

"Oh, they'll keep you forever."

He focused back on the highway. "How can you be so sure?"

"Well, Chief Rasband was Chief for something like twenty years. Maybe twenty-five."

"Huh." He slowed as a massive amount of cars came into view. "Is this it?"

Berlin couldn't believe they'd arrived already. Cole was right. This date was so much better than their last. "This is it. The parking lot is tiny, so anywhere along the road is fine."

He didn't seem to hear her, because he kept on driving. He pulled into the lot, and Berlin bit her tongue. He'd do what he wanted, no matter what she said.

Miraculously, as if someone had saved him a parking spot, there was an open space that he swung the car into. He turned and grinned at her. "You never said how old you were."

"Twenty-seven," she said. "My birthday is in October."

His smile widened and he said, "That's not too big of a gap, is it? I mean, a lot of people are a decade apart in age."

Berlin swallowed and licked her lips, wishing she could give up the nervous habit. Not only did her lipstick taste like dry cardboard, but she didn't like broadcasting her anxiety. "First, never say the word *decade* to describe it. Ten years seems much smaller. Second, I've...dated men older than you. When I was younger."

His eyebrows shot sky high. "Is that so?"

Berlin lifted one shoulder in a shrug meant to say *It's no big deal.* But her family had thought so. Caitlyn, Scotty, everyone at church. They all seemed to have an opinion about it, and though Berlin had liked Gray, their age difference was something neither of them could get past. That, and his teenage daughter.

"So ten years—nine really—is okay with me."

"Great," he said. "It's okay with me too." He got out of the car and came around to open her door.

"Who was the guy you dated that was much older than you?"

Berlin cleared her throat. This was normal conversation. He naturally would be curious about her past relationships. She reminded herself that this was what people did when they dated. They talked about themselves. Got to know one another. Made compromises.

"Um, it was Gray. Gray Salisbury? He's a detective with the Unified Police. They work with our PD all the time."

Cole stared at her for a moment past comfortable and then he sent his booming laughter into the summer sky. He was still chuckling when he said, "Wow. You and Gray."

"He's a great guy."

"Of course, yeah, sure." Cole took her hand in his and walked toward the front of the building. "He has a kid, doesn't he?"

"Oh, you're no good at asking questions you already know the answer to." She bumped him with her hip.

"How far apart are you in age?"

"A decade."

He paused before opening the door. "Wow, when you say it like that, it doesn't sound like long at all."

"Ha ha." Berlin rolled her eyes and nodded toward the door. "Have you been here before?"

"Nope."

"It can be loud. Better brace yourself."

He opened the door and sure enough, a wall of sound spilled out. The band had already started, and the entire lobby teemed with people, most of them couples, waiting for tables. Cole stepped right up to the hostess podium and leaned against it like he owned the place. Berlin hadn't noticed his cowboy boots when he'd picked her up, but she saw them now. Oh, how she hoped he could dance.

She recognized the band playing as Wild West Hearts, and they played a variety of ballads and quick pieces meant for line dances. A cheer went up from the stage area, and people flocked to the cleared area to dance.

Berlin watched them with eagerness, bouncing on the balls of her feet. Cole's hand slipped back into hers, startling her.

"All set?" He tugged on her fingers.

"We're ready already?"

"I told you I'd get a reservation." He didn't seem to notice the way everyone nearby gawked at them, so Berlin pressed her lips together and went with him. Once they were seated in a booth, with menus, and the overly bubbly hostess gone, Berlin leaned forward.

"I know they don't take reservations here, Cole."

He flicked her a glance over the top of the menu. "I pulled a few strings."

"What kind of strings?"

"Why does it matter?"

Berlin exhaled and glanced at the couples dancing to a romantic song that featured the fiddle and an accordion. "I guess it doesn't."

"Just like it doesn't matter that you go to church and I don't, or that you don't eat meat and I think a meal without meat isn't really a meal."

Berlin's mind whined with all he'd said at once. Sudden realization hit her, and she physically fell back against the upholstered booth. "That was why you were in bad mood on Sunday."

He sighed and put his menu down, apparently giving up on searching it while they were talking. "Why's that?"

"You tell me."

A waitress approached before he could say a word, and they put in their drink orders and asked for a few more minutes with the menu.

"All right," he said, covering the menu with his forearms and leaning into them. "Yes, I was a little put off by the...differences between us. It seemed like we didn't have anything in common."

"That's not a terrible thing," Berlin said.

"I realize that." He picked up the menu. "Now." He deliberately blew his breath out, a signal that this conversation was over. "What's good here? I assume you've been here a lot."

She had, yes. She relaxed as she quizzed him if he

liked bleu cheese or Swiss, a rare steak or a medium burger, regular French fries or the sweet potato kind.

"See?" she said. "Another thing we share. Our love of sweet potato fries." She gave him a smile, glad when he returned it.

"Remember how I said I wasn't great at this?" He handed the menu to the waitress but kept his eyes on Berlin's. "Maybe I get a few do-overs?"

"Maybe." Berlin turned her attention to the waitress and put in her order—the pulled pork sandwich with the spicy barbecue sauce. Cole ordered a rib eye, medium-rare, and a double order of the sweet potato fries.

"You know what would make this date amazing?" Berlin took a small sip of her soda.

Cole folded his arms and gave her an inquisitive look. "What?"

"Dancing."

CHAPTER 6

C ole could barely eat, what with the promise of dancing after they finished. He wasn't sure why he'd promised Berlin anything of the sort. But she'd looked so hopeful and happy, and he didn't want this date ending the way the last one had.

"So you work for your family," he said. "Tell me more about that."

Berlin lit up, her love for her family obvious. "I'm the accountant for the company. I took most of my classes online, and then I finished up the last two years on-campus in Colorado."

"How long have you been back in town?"

"Oh, about a year." She took a bite of her sandwich and while she chewed, her fingers snuck across the middle of the table and took a few of his fries.

Something sparked in him. It felt like it was their twentieth date, not their second. And certainly not their second after a disastrous first. Sharing food. Teasing. Talking about life. Cole hadn't known dating could be like this.

"I have eight brothers and sisters," she said. "I'm the youngest."

"Eight, wow."

"Surely you've heard of the Fullers."

He shook his head. "Should I have? You guys big lawbreakers or something?"

"Well, my brother-in-law is one of your men."

"Oh, yeah? Who?"

"Tate Benson. He's married to my oldest sister." Berlin watched him, almost like she didn't believe he didn't know everything about everyone in her family. She had no idea how much he worked, and Cole would need to tell her at some point. He'd taken the job in Brush Creek, because he adored small western towns. He loved hiking, fishing, and camping, and he'd though those hobbies would be a perfect way to unwind after a busy day at the station.

But he mostly just collapsed on the couch with his dogs on the floor to unwind. If he even made it home. At least he'd cleaned up the evidence of his sleeping in his office before Berlin had come that morning.

"I like Tate," he said. The man had certainly never given him any trouble. "Good cop."

"She runs the office. You probably spoke to her to arrange your lawn care."

"Probably." Cole could remember tiny details, sometimes things he'd seen in a photo or a crime scene once. He was great with names too. But who he spoke with to arrange his yard work two years ago wasn't in his repertoire.

Berlin sighed and looked down at her food. Cole regretted his snappy response and decided to do something he hadn't done before. "So I grew up in Dallas. My parents still live there."

He talked about himself for the rest of the meal, giving her little things about where his brothers were and what they did for a living.

"Wait. So none of you are married?" Berlin seemed shocked by such a thing.

"That's right."

"All of my brothers and sisters are married." Her voice carried a wistful quality that even the loud music couldn't cover up. He had no idea what to say to bring back the fun, flirty Berlin that called to his soul.

So he threw down his napkin and asked, "Wanna dance?"

Her gaze flew to his. "Really?"

"I can't promise I won't stomp your feet to smithereens," he said, scooting to the edge of the seat and standing. "But I think you suggested this place hoping for dancing, and that's what you're gonna get."

Berlin laughed as she slipped her hand into his and practically danced her way onto the floor. He chuckled too, but he had no idea where to put his hands or how to move to the beat. Thankfully, Berlin seemed to be a natural, and she guided his palms to her waist, and gave directions for which way he should go and when he should twirl her.

They laughed, and he bumped into more than a few people, saying "Sorry," more than anything else. But he never stepped on her toes, and he considered that a huge win.

The music settled into a slow song, and Cole knew how to dance this way. He brought Berlin close to his chest, and she tucked herself right into his arms. Holding her felt magical and like the entire world had stopped spinning, leaving only he and Berlin rotating slowly to the piano and violin as they sang a sad song together.

She pulled back slightly and gazed up at him, a sparkle in her eye that he'd seen in women's eyes before. Funny thing was, he had the same electricity coursing through him, bending his back as he inched closer to Berlin.

Her eyes drifted closed, and Cole's did too. Somewhere outside this sphere where he and Berlin existed, the piano stopped playing. Didn't matter. What mattered was kissing her. Right now.

His mouth touched hers, and she pulled in a breath. In the next moment, someone bumped him, knocking him sideways, and he heard, "Sorry, Chief," as everything spun back to normal.

The slow song had ended. Around them, people were spinning and twirling, laughing and dancing to another song that was so fast, Cole felt sure he'd trample someone if he tried to do the steps.

So he tugged Berlin off the dance floor, feeling flushed and incomplete, desperate with want for that kiss he hadn't truly gotten.

Hours later, he walked her to her front door, where she turned and put one palm flat against his chest. "This was so much better than last time."

"I couldn't agree more." He looked at her hand. "I assume this means you don't want me to kiss you goodnight."

She licked those lips, driving him absolutely crazy, and the fearful edge in her eyes answered him well enough.

"Would you like to come to my father's retirement party?" she asked. "My whole family will be there, and it'll be insane." She laughed, but it didn't hold much merriment. "All of our clients are invited too. It's at my parents' house next weekend."

Cole could barely think past the next five minutes, especially if he wasn't going to get to kiss her goodnight. "I'll have to check my schedule, but I think I can make it work."

She put her second palm on his chest and leaned into him. "Great. Then you get your kiss." She stretched up and pressed her lips to his cheek, maybe a little lower than normal, and settled back on her feet.

"That's it?" he practically growled.

"You'll want to leave that growly-bear stuff in the

office when you come to the party." She backed away from him, the blush in her cheeks indicating that she wanted more than a quick swipe of her mouth against his jaw too.

"When can I see you again?" he asked as she twisted the doorknob to go inside.

"Next weekend. At the party." She waggled her fingers and disappeared inside, the door clicking closed and the lock sliding into place a very final note to a very good date.

Cole supposed it would have to do. He certainly wasn't going to bang down the door and demand she get back out there and kiss him. Even he had some limits.

Not many when it comes to her, he thought as he went back to his car and headed home.

———

COLE WAS sure each day without seeing Berlin would be torture. It started out that way, but when he wanted to call her, he called his mother instead. When he wanted to talk to her, he texted and enjoyed the back and forth banter they seemed to perfect after the first few days.

The weekend wasn't slow at the station, not with summer in full swing now. It seemed Oxbow Park hosted a different event every night, and officers were needed to patrol the pathways, the forests surrounding the lake, and the traffic situations.

Cole took his turn on the evening events, the same as

anyone else. He spent hours filling out payroll paper-work, responding to phone calls, and dealing with sched-ules, shift changes, and dozens of personalities.

He brought Sarge and Honor to work as often as possible, otherwise the two shepherds would never get out of the house. So it was that Wednesday night found him showing up to his Boy Scout meeting with the German shepherds in tow.

The six thirteen-year-olds loved the dogs, and he had them sit and wait before he allowed the boys to say hello. He couldn't help the pride that swelled his chest as he watched his dogs accept the love from the teens. He loved his work with the boys, and they seemed to like him too.

He'd taught them how to take care of dogs, and he'd shown them basic canine training using Sarge and Honor. Tonight, though, it was all about Flag Day and tomorrow's work.

"All right, boys," he said. "Over here." They gathered around where he sat at a metal picnic table, at a pavilion in the park. "We have over five hundred flags to put up by eight a.m. That's about one hundred each." He glanced around at his guys. "So Barlow, you wanna split us up?"

The almost-fourteen-year-old took over, drawing red lines around certain blocks in town and assigning routes to various boys.

"We'll meet at my house tomorrow," Cole said. "What time, do you think?" He really wanted the boys to have ownership of what they did. He'd never liked it when his parents had bossed him around or feeling like he was being forced to do something against his will.

"The flags should be up by eight, right?" Barlow looked around at the other boys. "So six?"

"I'll get doughnuts and chocolate milk," Cole offered. "We can load up and go." He glanced at the notes on his phone. "I've got Chance's dad coming to drive. And Arnie's. And Sebastian, your mom said she could fit some in her sedan." Cole wondered briefly if he could call Berlin. Ask her to ride along with him while he supervised thirteen-year-olds on Flag Day.

Before he could decide, it was time to move on, talk about the proper care and handling of the flag, and then he brought out the chocolate bars he'd bought for their meeting. He'd learned after only one week that food was a requirement to get boys to show up for scouts. And he wanted the boys to come, really enjoyed his time with them, though it was one more thing on his never-ending to-do list.

Just as the meeting ended and he was rooting around in his SUV to find a ball or two to throw to Sarge and Honor, his phone sounded. He checked it to find Berlin's name on the screen. He tapped her name and found a photo loading.

This was new. She hadn't texted him any photos, and he ignored Sarge's whines as he waited. The image finally came up to show her with four blonde women—clearly her sisters. Another text came through, and it said *I told my sisters about you. I mean, they know who you are, but I told them we were sort of seeing each other.*

"Sort of seeing each other?" Cole tapped the message on the screen. *Is that what we're doing?*

And maybe slipping a bit into his beast mode, he added *Can I see you tonight?* which hopefully she correctly interpreted as *Can I kiss you when I see you tonight?*

Can't, she said. *Fuller family dinner every Wednesday. We're finalizing everything for the party on Saturday. You're still coming, right?*

He'd told her every day since last Friday that he was coming. Why she kept asking, he wasn't sure.

Can I call you? he texted. He wanted to ask her, but he also just wanted to hear her voice.

She didn't answer right away, so he went back to his search for a ball, finally coming up with a ratty tennis ball that Sarge would love. Cole held it up with an "A-ha!" and sure enough Sarge whined. Even Honor lay halfway down on her haunches, ready to launch herself after the object.

He threw the ball and watched the shepherds tear after it. Sarge was the faster of the pair of dogs, and he almost always beat Honor. He was an excellent catch too, usually snagging the ball out of the air no matter how low it bounced. Sometimes, though, he bobbled it, allowing her to snatch it from under his nose.

He threw the ball over and over, waiting for Berlin to

text him back. She never did, and when he realized how thirsty his dogs where, he loaded them up and took them home.

Later that night, when he should've been in bed already because the boys were coming the next morning at six, his phone rang. Because of his job, he never put it on silent, and he looked at the name on the screen, the letters blurry before his eyes. He could still see *Berlin* clearly enough, and he hurried swipe open the call.

"Hey," he said, his voice a little froggy from exhaustion, a smile on his face.

"Sorry I didn't answer earlier," she said. "My mom came over, and she's pretty freaky about having phones out during the family dinner."

Cole chuckled and asked, "How old are you again?"

"You haven't met my mom."

"No, I haven't." He relaxed back into the couch. "It's so good to hear your voice."

"I was thinking maybe we could get together tomorrow. You know, I should prep you to meet my family. They're...loud and crazy."

"Ah, just what I like."

She laughed and said, "Yeah, right. I told my sisters I'd give you ten minutes before you bolted on Saturday."

"Is that why you keep asking me if I'm going to come?"

"I—do I?"

"Every day, Berlin." He liked saying her name and he

grinned at the ceiling. "I'm sure it'll be crazy. But I can handle it."

"You sure?"

"What are you really worried about?"

"Nothing," she said, but there was something there. Something she wasn't saying. Cole had a lie-o-meter and it was singing right now.

His first instinct was to call her on it, but then he thought about what Jordan and Mason would tell him. Their voices entered his head, and he simply said, "All right. Tomorrow night? You want to go dancing again?" He sincerely hoped not, but if he could see her again, he'd do almost anything.

"No, I was thinking of something a little more casual. Away from the crowds."

So he could kiss her. "Yeah, sure," he said, maybe a little too eagerly.

She laughed, the sound carefree and wonderful, just like in his office. "See? You are a hermit."

"I am not. I've directed traffic twice this week for huge events at the park, and I just did Boy Scouts tonight —with six teenagers."

"Oh, wow, that's...intense."

"So what were you thinking for tomorrow?"

"I was thinking maybe you'd let me cook for you."

Cole sat up, pure surprise pulling through him. "Sounds great. Your place?"

"My place. Seven o'clock."

"I'll be there."

"You can bring your dogs. I have a big backyard that's fenced."

"Deal." He hung up, happier than he'd been in a long time. Tomorrow at seven couldn't come fast enough.

CHAPTER 7

Berlin bustled around the kitchen, flipping the chicken fried steaks and checking the timer on the pot of potatoes. Everything looked good. The scent of fried food filled the house as she set two plates on the table.

It had been Fabi's idea to invite Cole for dinner. Berlin hadn't told her sisters everything, but Wren would not leave her alone about the police chief coming to haul boxes in for her last week. So Berlin had mentioned they'd gone to dinner, and things had snowballed from there.

At least she hadn't kissed him yet. Every cell in her body burned to do exactly that, but she didn't want to push things too fast with him. All of her sisters agreed that ten years—nine really, come October—wasn't too old, especially because he hadn't been married before and had no kids.

With silverware beside plates, and glasses in position, she turned back to the stove. The timer on the potatoes went off and she hurried to check their doneness and then drained them, a huge plume of steam rising and giving her a facial she didn't need.

She'd deliberately stayed out of the bathroom so she wouldn't touch up her makeup. Her false eyelashes itched almost constantly, and Caitlyn said that was normal for someone wearing them for the first time. Berlin wanted to rip them all off, but it was more painful than she'd thought. So she'd quit after the first few, hoping she didn't look too ridiculous with a few less lashes on her right eye.

The clock ticked to seven, and knocking sounded on her front door, almost like Cole had snuck into her house and synced his clock to hers and then set a timer.

"It's open!" she called as she turned back to the chicken fried steaks. They looked glorious and golden, and she lifted one out of the bubbling oil to check the doneness. Thirty more seconds.

The door opened, breaking the seal on the house, and Cole walked in. He was powerful and gorgeous, wearing jeans and a T-shirt, that cowboy hat and a ten-gallon smile. "Wow, smells good in here."

His two dogs came after him, ever the obedient shepherds. They frolicked with her two pups, and he opened the back door to let them all out into the yard, chuckling as they went in a scraping of claws and the panting of tongues.

Then he moved into the kitchen and slipped his hands along her waist, almost making her drop the last chicken fried steak before she could add it to the others already draining on the paper towels.

She finished the job, laughing, and turned in his arms. "I hope you like chicken fried steak."

He held her close, almost swaying with her to music only he could hear. "Oh, I do." He swept his hat off his head and leaned down. "I really wanted to kiss you last weekend. Can we start with that tonight so I don't go crazy?"

Shocked by his forward manner and blunt way of speaking exactly what he was thinking, Berlin took a few seconds to blink at him.

"Please?" he added, his eyes drifting closed and his face dipping lower, the tip of his nose brushing her cheek.

Berlin let her eyes close too, and the moment between them turned soft, intimate, and wonderful. She swayed with him, her hands slipping up his arms and across his biceps to the back of his neck.

"Berlin?"

She didn't have the mental energy to respond, as every sense was heightened to the touch, the smell, the flavor of this man. She made contact with his mouth first, a quick brush of her lips against his.

White lights popped behind her eyes, and she swayed on her feet, an action completely separate from the way he still drifted left and right with her. He kissed her tenderly, softly, like he was afraid he might break her.

She lifted up on her toes and *kissed* him, eliciting a moan from somewhere deep in his core. He deepened the kiss, and Berlin wondered how she could ever cook in this kitchen again without reliving the best kiss of her life.

HOURS LATER, after they'd eaten, and held hands on the back porch as they watched the dogs run and play, and kissed on her couch, she lay in bed, her phone pressed to her ear. He'd left her house twenty minutes ago, but she couldn't help calling him.

He didn't seem confused or annoyed by the call, and she'd somehow unlocked the chatty version of Cole tonight. Maybe it had been the kiss. Or the phenomenal chicken fried steak. No matter what, she liked listening to him talk about his brothers and his job, his men and his dogs.

Finally, she said, "So we never talked about my family and the party."

"Oh, right. I'm sure I'll be fine, Berlin." He practically purred her name, and Berlin turned on her side and giggled, as if she were fourteen talking to her first boyfriend and not twenty-seven and dealing with a man a decade older than her.

"Have you met someone's family before?"

"Well, no."

So he'd never had a really serious relationship.

"Have you?" he asked.

"Just this one guy. We were getting pretty serious, I guess."

"Have you had a lot of boyfriends?"

Berlin hadn't anticipated this conversation turning to that. "A fair few," she admitted. "But you really take the prize. Number one, you're employed. Number two, I know your last name. Number three, you don't have a beard longer than my hair. So." She waved her hand around like he was there and could see her nonchalance.

He chuckled, and she wished she were curled up against his chest to feel the vibrations, the way she'd been earlier. "Wow, if I'd have known that was all it took, I may have started dating earlier."

"I've only left town for a couple of years," she said, feeling a bit defensive. "And the selection in Brush Creek isn't huge."

"And yet all eight of your siblings managed to get married."

"Ouch," she said, adding a laugh to the statement. But how could he know that was a sensitive subject for her? She hadn't told him, and he probably would've said it even if she had. *Not true*, she corrected herself. Cole could come off as intimidating and commanding at first. And he definitely spoke his mind. But so did Berlin, and she wasn't interested in playing games with her love life, so she found his sometimes cringe-worthy statements somewhat refreshing—as long as they weren't about her makeup or her marital status.

"Sorry," he said. "Sometimes I say...I won't do that on Saturday. Best behavior."

"I'm wondering if you want to come as my boyfriend or simply a client of the company." Berlin clenched her eyes closed and hoped he'd say boyfriend.

"What do you want me to do?"

"Well, seeing as how you couldn't wait to kiss me tonight, I think you coming as my boyfriend would be fine. I mean, my sisters kind of already know we're dating, and my parents will be really busy anyway, so...."

"Couldn't wait to kiss you?"

"Well, yeah." She laughed. "It was a great night, Cole. If you don't want to play the boyfriend at the party, I'm okay with it."

"Berlin." Something came through the line from his end, maybe a chair scraping the floor, maybe something else. "I'm not playing anything here."

Berlin closed her eyes as a rush of warmth filled her.

"Are you?" he asked.

Her eyes flew open. "Of course not."

"Then I'll be your boyfriend at the party...and around town...and when we go out."

"What about church?" All her siblings had someone to sit by at church, and Berlin was growing weary of sitting next to Wren just to help with her niece.

"Oh, well...."

"Come on," she said, somewhat teasing. "You're a

good ol' Southern boy. You expect me to believe your momma didn't make you go to church?"

"She did."

"But you don't go now."

"I sort of...fell out of the habit over the years."

"Maybe you'd like to fall back in, with me."

A pause came through the line, with only a single bark sounding in her ear. "Is that Honor?"

"She just needs to go out."

Berlin waited, knowing Cole would come back to what she'd said. At least she hoped so.

He exhaled. "Your faith is important to you." He wasn't asking.

"It is."

"I...was like that once. I could try it again."

Berlin's face exploded into a smile. "This Sunday?"

"What time?"

"Ten-thirty."

"You realize I'm on call. I might not be available every Sunday. All of that."

"I know, I know." She sat up and stroked Brownie and then Cocoa, who both lay on the end of her bed. "But I think it's important that we're on the same page with church before we go any farther."

"I'm okay with that," he said.

Berlin couldn't believe this gentle giant had been living in Brush Creek for two years and they hadn't met. Of course, she'd only been back in town for twelve months, but still.

"Thank you," she said. "I'll respect whatever you decide to do, but the pastor is really great. And the choir will blow your mind."

"Oh, wow. I think you said the same thing about your sister's potato salad, which I'll get to eat on Saturday. Maybe I won't make it to church." He laughed, and Berlin joined him before finally saying goodbye and falling back on her bed, her phone clutched to her chest.

As she laid there, she realized she'd never felt like this about anyone before. This level of spark, this many jitters just thinking about seeing him, this much *happiness* coursing through her. She'd heard her sisters talk about this feeling, but she hadn't truly understood it—until now.

"But you're not in love with him," she whispered to herself as she crawled beneath the comforter and snuggled in to bed. It was much too soon for that. But she felt herself slipping in that definite direction, much more than she ever had before, even with men where she'd had fantastic first dates and seemed to have a lot in common with.

"I guess we'll see, right guys?" she said to her dogs as they came to lie on either side of her. She fell asleep with fantasies of her and Cole holding hands as their four dogs ran through the park.

Chapter 8

Berlin stayed on Cole's mind every waking minute. While he filled out paperwork. While he joked with his officers. While he got a lecture from his secretary for not putting a flag out in front of her house on Flag Day.

He'd tried to explain to her that the scouts only did the homes that had signed up, but it was a fruitless argument. Lesli insisted she'd signed up, and Cole had personally put a flag on her front lawn on Friday by lunchtime.

He worked feverishly on Saturday morning, hoping to get ahead since he'd be gone for the party and then tomorrow for church too. He had good captains and lieutenants, and he didn't need to be at the station twenty-four-seven. He simply liked it. Had always lived that way. But he was starting to realize that if he wanted a relationship with Berlin—and he did—his work schedule had to be adjusted.

She'd asked him to come to her house and they'd go to the party together. When he arrived, the front door was open and her two dogs lay at the bottom of the steps, in a patch of shade from the trees edging her yard. He smiled at them, her cute pups bringing him a measure of joy that some would've classified as a bit crazy.

"Come on, guys. Go to the back." Both of his dogs rode in the front seat of the SUV, and Honor always went first, and Sarge waited for her to hop into the back seat. Cole got out and went around the back to open the rear door on the passenger side.

His dogs jumped down and hurried over to Berlin's, and the four canines circled each other for a minute. "Stay here, guys." His dogs wouldn't run off, and it didn't seem like Berlin's would either.

Cole climbed the front steps and peered inside. "Hey, anyone here?"

"In the bedroom!"

Well, that was one place he wouldn't be going. "So I'll take the dogs out back then?"

"Yes, please. I'm almost ready."

Cole turned back to the animals and said, "Come on, guys." His dogs came, and hers followed. When they were in the back and he'd seen the three bowls of water Berlin had already put out, he went back in the house.

Berlin came down the hall at the same moment, wearing a bright pink party dress. Her hair framed her face nicely. With her eyelashes and the copious amounts of makeup, she looked both sophisticated and soft, and Cole's breath stuck in his lungs.

"Well, look at you." He inched toward her, his fingers twitching to draw her close, hold her there, kiss her until he couldn't think straight. Of course, that was how he'd felt the other night after only one kiss.

"Too much makeup, I know." She flashed him a smile that was tight around the edges and picked up her keys.

"You're driving?" he asked. "I parked behind you."

"Oh, no." She put the keys back on the kitchen counter. "I'm not driving." She smoothed down her skirt and looked around. "Okay, um."

Cole smiled at her nerves—it was nice to see her a little bit out of her element. Everything she did seemed to be flawless, even the fact that she'd claimed to be almost a quarter of the way finished with the police audit after only a week.

He drew her into an embrace and said, "Just breathe, sweetheart. It's just a family party."

"It's my father's retirement party," she clarified as she pressed her cheek to his chest. "It's a very big deal for us."

While Cole couldn't really understand, he said he could. "Just tell me what to do, and I'll do it," he added.

"Just hold my hand on the way in," she said. "Stay close to me."

"Hold your hand. Stay close." He hooked his thumb toward her back door. "Dogs secure."

She looked up at him and stretched up to kiss him. This was a chaste union of their mouths, and he felt her need to simply anchor herself. So he let her set the pace, and he gave her whatever she needed. She ended the sweet kiss and rested her forehead against his collarbone.

"All right." Berlin drew in a deep breath. "Let's go."

The drive from her place to her parent's only took a few minutes, and she talked about her grandparents. She'd mentioned them last night, as it had been her grandmother who'd taught her how to cook. She'd spoken of them with fondness, and Cole found himself wanting to be part of a family again.

He spoke to his parents, his brothers, fairly regularly. But it wasn't the same as having someone to get together with on the weekends, after work, or just when he didn't want to be alone.

Cole had never thought he would have a problem with going home alone. But the more time he spent with Berlin, the more he disliked his quiet house and empty office.

"Pull over here," she said, and he eased to a stop behind another SUV. "We'll have to walk." She nodded toward a mansion at the end of the street, only about a hundred yards away. "It's not far, but it seems like all of my siblings beat us here."

"We're not late, are we?" He unbuckled and got out of the car, alarm blipping through him.

"No, we're fifteen minutes early." She met him at the front corner of the hood. "Welcome to the Fuller family."

She gave him that strained smile, and he slipped his hand into hers.

They walked down the street and up the circle driveway to the front door. Berlin went inside, and Cole expected a wall of noise to hit him, the way it had at Teddy's. But it was fairly quiet just inside the doors.

"Grams," Berlin said. "What're you doing in here?" She stepped to the left, where a sitting room provided a good escape from the rest of the house.

The old woman looked up at Berlin, a weathered smile wrinkling her face. "Oh, Berlin. I was sent to wait for you." She stood, using the arm of the chair to steady herself. "You must be Cole."

Surprise streamed through him, but he stepped forward and shook the woman's hand. "I am. And you must be...." He tossed a glance at Berlin, but she didn't come to his rescue. "Grandma Ebony, yes?"

A smile touched her lips again. "I wasn't really sent here to wait for Berlin." Her blue eyes sparkled like cold diamonds.

"No?" He chuckled. "Are you telling me I don't want to go into the backyard?" If anyone ever asked, he'd lie about the slight trepidation tripping through him.

"Oh, my daughter expects perfection from imperfect humans." Grandma Ebony took his hand between both of hers. "She should be calmed down by now. After all, the guests will be here soon."

"Come with us," Berlin said, linking her arm through her grandmother's. "And I guess you know Cole."

"The Chief of Police." Her grandmother moved forward with Berlin, and Cole went behind them. The house had a personal touch to it, with family pictures and whimsical décor on the walls. It seemed her mother loved Paris or France, as there were multiple items in French or with the Eiffel Tower on them.

The kitchen was massive, with pictures of grandchildren stuck to the fridge with colorful, homemade magnets. Again, a pinch of yearning hit him for something he didn't have—didn't even know he wanted.

Maybe his mama had been right to badger him and his brothers about getting married and giving her some grandbabies.

They moved through the kitchen and through a set of double French doors which led into an outdoor kitchen. These Fuller's had some serious money, and Cole's muscles tightened as Grandma Ebony stumbled a bit on the cobblestone steps. His hand flew out to steady her, and Berlin gave him a grateful look.

"Stay on the path, Grams," she said. Berlin approached a long picnic table with dozens of chairs surrounding it. A few people sat at the picnic table, but most of them hung out in the camp chairs and loungers. Kids ran on the expansive lawn, way out by the tall trees, and dozens of round tables had been set up in the space in between.

A blonde woman—clearly the one in charge—said something to a couple of other women, and they went to do whatever she'd said. Berlin's mother.

"There you go. Sit here by Gramps." Berlin leaned over and gave her grandfather a kiss, then slipped her hand back into Cole's. The older man followed her movement and looked up at them. "Do you guys know Cole Fairbanks?" She squeezed his hand, and Cole put on his most charming smile, the one he used whenever he had to make a public appearance and wanted to come off as friendly.

"Nice to meet you," he said, shaking her grandfather's hand. He surveyed the party, checking for ways into the yard and ways out before he realized he wasn't working security at this event.

"Aunt Berlin!" A swarm of kids ran toward them, and Berlin laughed as she swept a couple of the smaller ones into her arms.

"I got a new puppy," one of them said while another told her about an art project he was doing for his preschool class. She spoke to all of them, handed out hugs like they grew on trees, and then everyone sort of stilled and every eye focused on him.

"Hey," he said, kids completely outside of his wheelhouse. Berlin had mentioned nieces and nephews, but Cole was utterly unprepared to deal with them.

"This is my boyfriend," she said. "Cole."

"He's a police officer," one of the older boys said.

Cole crouched in front of him. "How do you know?" He wore his cowboy hat and casual clothes.

"You came to my school," the boy said simply. "You had your dogs." He glanced around like Cole would've brought two German shepherds to a retirement party. "You don't have them here, do you?"

Cole laughed and tousled the kid's hair. "Nope. But I take 'em to the park a lot. Maybe I'll see you there."

The boy's face lit up and he said, "All right. Cool," before running off.

Cole straightened and watched them all follow him before turning back to Berlin. She looked at him with wonder on her face, and he said, "What?"

"You go to schools?"

"All the time." He shrugged and stuffed his hands in his pockets. "I mean, not here, because there's only like, four schools here, but yeah."

She slid her hands up his chest, obviously forgetting where she was. Still, his blood tingled in his veins and he couldn't look away from her.

"What else do you do that I don't know about?"

A lot of things, actually, but he thought he'd save the boring staff meetings and gun safety classes for another time. Instead, he said, "Boy Scouts."

"You're a Boy Scout?"

"I am. But I meant I'm a Scout leader now. I work with thirteen-year-olds. That flag on your parents' front yard? My boys did that."

Berlin looked impressed, and before he knew it, she'd stretched up and kissed him. Kissed him like they were alone and not standing in the middle of a party, with dozens of witnesses.

He cleared his throat and stepped back despite the

fact that everything in him wanted to keep kissing her. "Okay." He chuckled and glanced around. He was used to having a lot of people looking at him, but this felt different. These people were her siblings, her parents, her friends.

"Hey, Chief."

He spun to find a familiar face. Finally. "Milt." The relief in Cole's voice could've been heard in the next county over. He shook the man's hand. "Good to see you."

Milt looked to where Berlin stood behind Cole. "And you. I wasn't sure you'd be able to make it." His gaze wandered back to Cole, and his blue eyes were sharp.

"Yeah. I'm...well, I'm here with your sister."

Milt's jaw twitched. "I saw."

Humiliation ran through Cole and he couldn't help the way his own jaw clenched. He had no idea what to say, but it didn't matter. Milt stepped past him and gave Berlin a hug that lasted entirely too long. When he finally stepped away, he didn't look back and Berlin had turned the color of a ripe tomato.

Cole suddenly wanted nothing more than to leave this party. At least he'd already lasted more than ten minutes. He sighed and turned away, wondering what in the world had possessed Berlin to kiss him so intimately in front of *every*one.

"I'm sorry." She stepped to his side, her voice barley reaching his ears. She didn't touch him, and he felt a gulf between them now where there'd been nothing before.

"Should I go?" He spoke without moving his mouth.

She sighed and gestured to three women striding toward him, one of which would be delivering a baby soon.

"You can't." She looked up at him and then back to the approaching women. "Those are three of my sisters."

CHAPTER 9

Berlin had never felt so foolish, even when she'd endured a family party where her mom and dad tag-teamed her about Gray's age and how she was in no way fit to be a mother to a teenager at age twenty-three.

There had been a lot of questions and threats of pulling her tuition money and the whole family had witnessed it. Thankfully, Berlin had been able to go back to Colorado Springs to finish her last year of college, and well, her parents had been right.

And here she was again, parading around a man ten years older than her. Kissing him in front of the whole party. Her stomach twisted, and she could barely breathe.

The stiff way Cole held his body indicated that he was furious with her and barely holding it together. She expected the beast to appear at any moment, but he shook hands with Wren, Fabi, and Jazzy, looking between the twins a couple of times.

"Different hair," he said. "Let's see. Berlin said Fabi has the short hair." He flashed a look at her but their eyes didn't truly meet. "Right?"

"Right on, Chief." Fabi gave him a warm smile and then looked at Berlin with all kinds of statements in her gaze. "Can I steal you away for a second, Berlin?"

"Oh, I—"

"Two minutes." Fabi latched onto her with the strength of alligator jaws, and Berlin tossed a helpless glance at Cole. But he didn't even look at her. Definitely mad about the kiss. As he should be.

"What are you doing?" Fabi hissed as she walked.

Berlin considered playing dumb, but too much teemed inside for her to blow off. "I don't know," she moaned. "He's just so...."

"Sexy?"

"Surprising," Berlin said. "I wasn't expecting him to be so personable." He'd been nice to her at the summer fair, sure. Even gone through with the date. But it had been a nightmare, a complete one-eighty from the following date.

"Well, sucking face with him in front of the grandparents was a bad choice."

"I just sort of lost my mind."

"Don't let Mom hear you say that, because she's already quite unhappy with the idea of you and Cole."

"Why? He's younger than Gray."

"Still a lot older than you."

"Neither of us cares about that." Berlin scanned the yard but couldn't find her mom. It didn't matter. Last time, she agreed with them about certain points when it came to Gray. But there was nothing she didn't feel right about when it came to Cole. She was an adult. She didn't need their permission to date a man. He was the *Chief* of *Police* for crying out loud.

"All right." Fabi turned back to the party, which had swelled by at least three dozen people, with more streaming around the house at a steady clip. "Oh, and Dahlia's pregnant." Fabi walked away before Berlin could fully decode the tone of voice her sister had used.

Berlin's stomach fell to the ground, and all she could feel was that she was getting further and further behind. Which made no sense. Dahlia was twelve years older than Berlin. *Twelve.* And just barely having her first child.

And life wasn't a race anyway.

"Attention!" Her mom had a microphone, and Berlin migrated back to Cole as her mother continued to get everyone's attention. He stood with Tate and Wren, Fabi and Ed, and Jazzy and Max. Berlin wanted to touch him, simply to ground herself, but she didn't dare. She felt like holding his hand right now would push him further from her instead of bringing him closer. So she put on her happy face and endured the party, hoping no one else would bring up her blunder.

TO COLE'S CREDIT, he stayed for the duration of the party. He drove her home and said he'd see her tomorrow. His still mask broke when he saw the dogs—the only time. He didn't kiss her goodbye, but did say he'd see her later.

Berlin had fully expected him to stand her up for church, probably through a text. But he showed up outside the red brick building twenty minutes early, and they sat way down on the end of the Fuller family bench. He didn't hold her hand or lift his arm around her shoulders, which left Berlin hollow and honestly a bit scared.

He'd turned into a numb beast instead of the fiery, snappy one she'd come to expect. She could handle the latter, but this iced over version of him she didn't know how to deal with.

Pastor Peters spoke about honesty and telling the truth, relating stories of businessmen and women who stood for what was right and were blessed for it.

Berlin had never been tested in that way. College had been easy, and she'd never felt the temptation to cheat. She hadn't had to interview for jobs, and she'd never really tasted of that level of competition before.

As she sat there, her leg barely touching Cole's, she realized how sheltered and spoiled her life had been. But that wasn't something she could control, and she didn't feel particularly bad about it.

She felt uninteresting. Why would someone as well-traveled and with experience in the FBI, with various police forces, and the Boy Scouts be interested in her?

She didn't do any charity work. She didn't work with youth. His job had to be ten times busier than hers, and he did much more than she did.

Pastor Peters started to wind down—Berlin had attended hundreds of his sermons, so she knew. She tapped Cole's arm and whispered, "I have to go."

He looked at her blankly for a moment and then nodded. Berlin couldn't stand to be beside him for another second and she practically exploded to her feet and hurried up the aisle.

She expected him to follow her out, but there were no bootsteps behind her. She waited in the lobby, and he still didn't come. Bitter, and with a sob in her throat, she turned her back on the chapel and exited the building as quickly as her heels would take her.

Leaving her car in the parking lot, she crossed the bridge to the park and walked at a steady clip under the trees. Her office was only a few blocks down, and by the time she arrived, she was sweaty and out of breath. After all, she didn't work out in heels, in ninety-degree weather.

Once behind the locked door of the building and inside the office space for A Jack of All Trades, she kicked off her heels and faced the boxes of financial documents she hadn't gone through yet.

She couldn't stand to think about Cole, but she couldn't stop doing exactly that. But if she could focus on something else, just for a little while, maybe an idea for what to do about him would present itself.

The first box she opened had more payroll reports. These were easy. She read them, recorded them, checked the procedures for overtime pay and reporting of inconsistencies of mistakes.

It was mind-numbing work but required her to pay attention to what each piece of paper said, which made it perfect for this Sunday afternoon when she couldn't find peace in her usual places.

Her phone rang a half an hour later, and she expected to see Cole's name on the screen. But it was Dawn.

Berlin hesitated just a bit too long before answering, and the call went to voicemail. Before she could silence her phone—because she really didn't want to talk to anyone today—it started ringing again.

Dawn. Again.

Blowing out a sigh, Berlin picked up the phone and answered the call. "I'm not really in the mood for talking today."

"Great," her second oldest sister said. "Neither am I. What I have is a literal vat of chicken noodle soup. Nana Reba made it for me and Taya, because we've been under the weather. I wondered if you wanted some."

Berlin's annoyance faded. "You aren't feeling well?"

"I'm almost out of the first trimester," she said. "Everyone says it will get better then." She exhaled, and Berlin could hear the exhaustion in her sister. "So, soup? I'll have McDermott bring it after he gets home from church."

So Dawn hadn't been in the chapel. Hadn't seen

Berlin's exit while Cole sat there and let her go. Come to think of it, she hadn't been in the backyard yesterday during Berlin's kisscapade either.

"I'm at the office right now," she said. "But he can leave it on my porch. Or take it inside. I'm sure I didn't lock the front door."

A few beats of silence put Berlin back on heightened alert.

"Hiding at the office today?"

"No," Berlin said quickly. "I'm doing the police department audit, and I've fallen behind." She'd fallen behind because of all the time she spent thinking about Cole, or the hours she spent with Cole.

"Hm. You want some company from a semi-sick pregnant lady?"

Berlin laughed, thinking back at how Dawn had removed herself from the family. She hadn't come to the family dinners for years, and then...something changed. Berlin didn't know what. She'd never asked, and she'd been preoccupied with her own life, if she were being honest.

Her parents had been riding her about her degree, and she'd been working full-time for the company, part-time at the grocery store, and doing online classes. She didn't want to go back to those days at all, but even she'd known about the change in Dawn.

And then she'd married McDermott, and they'd been building a nice, quiet life together.

"It's fine," she said to Dawn, pulling herself back to the present. "I'm okay here. I...want to be alone."

"Okay," Dawn said in a dubious voice. "But please let me know if you need company. I'll come."

"Thanks." Berlin smiled at the kindness in her sister and hung up the phone. She managed to silence it and get back to the documents before her mind took her down the path to thinking about Cole again.

Hours later, Berlin's throat felt like someone had poured sand down it. Her back ached, and her neck had a certifiable kink in it. She finished the last file in the third box she'd been through that day and stood, bracing both hands on her lower back as she stretched. A groan filled the air and all she could think about was getting a drink.

She left the office and entered the front of the office where the tall reception counter sat. Wren usually worked there, and through a door behind her station was a little kitchen. The two women kept it stocked with water and all their favorite sodas. Wren usually had a cake in there too, with a couple different flavors of ice cream.

Berlin just wanted water, but she hadn't made it through the door leading into the kitchen when pounding sounded on the glass behind her.

Her heart catapulted to the back of her throat and adrenaline spiked through her blood. Her stomach swooped and she spun toward the sound, fear flowing through her like fast-moving water.

A tall figure had his hands splayed against the glass.

When he saw she was looking, he gestured for her to come let him in.

Berlin backed up, feeling for the doorway behind her. She'd left her phone in her office, so she ducked behind the tall counter and picked up the landline there. She had the first number dialed when she heard, "It's Cole, Berlin. And it's raining. You wanna let me in?"

She replaced the receiver in the cradle and straightened. She hadn't realized how dark it had gotten, as focused on her work as she was. She had no idea how much time had gone by, or why Cole was there. He obviously hadn't wanted to talk, or he would've followed her out of the chapel.

Stepping toward the doors to let him into the building, she thought *he's here to break up with you*. She squared her shoulders and prepared herself mentally and emotionally to hear him say it wasn't going to work out between them.

Her heart flopped around inside her chest like a rubber chicken, but she got the door unlocked. Cole burst into the building, bringing the scent of rain and cologne with him. He did not look happy, though he was definitely on another level of good-looking with wet hair and that dangerous glint in his dark eyes.

"I've called you half a dozen times." He slicked water off his bare arms. "And I've been looking for you for hours. I almost called in a missing persons."

Berlin scoffed as a sliver of guilt embedded into her heart. Maybe she shouldn't have silenced her phone. "I'm fine," she said around the dryness in her throat. "Thirsty, but fine." She moved past him, her bare feet touching some of the water that had dripped off him. "And I went through three more of your boxes." It was amazing how much she could get done when she wasn't obsessing about an upcoming dinner with Cole, or when she'd get to see Cole again, or how it felt to be kissed by Cole.

She entered the kitchen, her skin itching just from being in the same space as Cole. Not itching. Tingling. Tingling with anticipation. After pulling out a bottle of water, she opened it and drank almost the whole thing before turning to face him.

"Just get it over with," she said.

Cole had the decency to look confused. "Get what over with?"

Berlin folded her arms, the plastic bottle crinkling in a way that made her cringe. "If you're going to break up with me, just say it, and let's move on." She could be blunt too, if she had to be.

Cole's mouth dropped open slightly and then he tipped his head back and had the audacity to laugh. The sound sounded joyful and bright, loud and booming as it filled her ears and the office around her.

She finished her water and smashed the bottle into a little disc before replacing the cap. The noise got him to quiet, and his gaze burned into Berlin like a laser. "I'm not here to break up with you."

"No?"

He shook his head and paced further into the

kitchen. He leaned against the counter and crossed his arms too. "I was mad yesterday, because you'd gotten me all...all worked up about the party, and meeting some of your family members, and being on my best behavior—"

"I never said you needed to be on your best behavior." Berlin took a deep breath, gulping at the air. "*You* said you'd do that."

His expression darkened. "And then you're the one that made me look bad."

She had no defense against his accusation. "I made a mistake." Her voice sounded like she'd inhaled helium, and she turned away as her eyes began to burn. She would not cry in front of him. "I'm sorry. I just...you'd just...." She'd simply found him so attractive in that moment, with him being kind to her grandparents, and crouching down in front of her nieces and nephews, and learning he volunteered his time with teen boys.

She twisted back to him and employed her strength. "I'm sorry."

He gazed at her evenly, that muscle in his jaw jumping. Then he pushed away from the counter and approached her. Before she could think, or move, or even take another breath, he cradled her face in both of his hands and said, "All right," before kissing her like it was the first time.

Chapter 10

Cole wasn't sure what he was doing. He *had* come to the office building to break up with Berlin. Or at least he'd started out looking to find her to do exactly that.

But as the hours had dragged on, and he hadn't been able to find her, the panic driving him to keep looking couldn't be ignored. The thought of never seeing her again had his blood burning like lava and his nerves firing too quickly.

And as he kissed her now, all the same things were happening but for the opposite reason. Because she was his, and though she'd made a mistake at her parent's party, she'd owned it. Admitted it. Apologized for it.

And that was a really good thing in Cole's book, making Berlin ten times as attractive as he'd found her previously.

He finally pulled away, the taste of her in his mouth

now, and he wiped his lips. "Okay, so I saw some soup at your place, and I'm starving."

"You went in my house?"

"It's on the front porch, though…yeah, I went inside. You left your car at the church. You could've been anywhere." He shook his head, remembering the panic when he'd checked every room in her house and found them empty. He'd tried a couple of her sisters and even gone to her parents' house.

Her mother had not been overly welcome, but her father said she sometimes went into work on Sunday if she was stressed. And with the audit, Cole had decided to try one more place before going back to the station and filing that missing persons report.

Berlin backed out of his arms, and Cole let her go. He was not used to having his feelings and life wrapped up in another person, and he wasn't sure how he felt about it. He wasn't even sure when it had happened. He and Berlin were still at the beginning of their relationship.

"I don't want my sister's chicken noodle soup."

Cole watched her gather her dark hair into a ponytail. "Why'd you dye your hair?" He wasn't sure why he'd asked now, why it mattered.

Her eyes flew to his. "I, well, I was ready to do something different to get a different result. My friends said I should start with my appearance."

"Do you like it?"

She laughed darkly. "Not at all, but Starlee said it

would be hard to reverse, so I'm going to let it grow out a little and then have her fix it up."

Cole didn't want her to go back to her office and do any more work that day. "I can make grilled cheese sandwiches," he said. "I'd like to talk to you about church." He'd felt something there that had been missing in his life.

Berlin turned back to him again. "Church?"

"I need food first," he said. "I skipped lunch, because I was looking for you."

Her expression pinched, and Cole regretted his words. "It's fine. I just…let's go across the street to my place. We can talk and eat there."

Thankfully, Berlin didn't argue. It took her several minutes to get ready to go, and Cole waited on a sleek black leather couch in the lobby, trying to gather his thoughts together into something that made sense. For maybe the first time in his life, he wasn't exactly sure what he was doing. He'd been focused on his career for so long, and he always knew the next step to take for that.

What job to take. When to enroll in the FBI training class. Where to move.

But he had no idea what he was doing with Berlin.

Be honest. The pastor's words had settled in Cole's ears and meant something. He remembered how good he'd felt going to church with his family as he grew up. Sure, he'd gotten busy, but as he'd listened to the sermon, his heart had told him he needed to make time to feed his spirit, the same way he exercised, fed, and took care of his physical body.

Berlin appeared in the doorway of her office, now wearing her shoes. "Ready?"

Cole stood and said, "Ready," though he had no idea what he was doing. He extended his hand toward her, relieved when she slipped her fingers between his. It felt like they were starting over—for the third time. Cole didn't mind, especially if he could have another first kiss with Berlin.

———

JUNE WARMED and melted into July. The summer concert series started in the park, forcing Cole to bring in temporary officers to keep the patrols staffed and his full-time officers from banking too many overtime hours. With the audit going on, the last thing he needed was proof that he wasn't careful with the budget.

The public wouldn't like it if there weren't cops in the park either, so Cole did his best to show the people he was working for the town and keep his officers healthy and happy.

He attended as many events on Independence Day as possible, ending the day lying on his back with Berlin curled into his side as they watched the fireworks explode over the town of Brush Creek.

Cole attended church each week, no matter if that meant he had to sacrifice sleep to keep up with his police work, his exercise regime, and spending time with Berlin. Though he burned the candle at both ends, he felt happier than he'd ever been.

So happy, in fact, he called his mother one day in late July to let her know everything that had gone on in his life for the past eight weeks.

"Ma," he said. "It's your favorite son."

She laughed, the way she always did when he claimed to be her favorite. Yes, he'd spoken to her every week, and yes, she'd continued to badger him about "finding a girl" and "settling down" and "having babies."

He and Berlin hadn't spoken about children yet, and she hadn't invited him to any more family functions. The closest he got was sitting next to her at church, a row or two behind her siblings, grandparents, and parents.

"What're you up to?" His mom had the strongest Texas accent in the world, and it made Cole smile.

"Actually, I have some news for you."

"You're engaged."

"Mom." Now whatever he said would be much less impressive.

"You're not moving again, are you?"

"No, Mom. But I am dating someone."

She squealed, causing him to pull the phone away from his ear so he wouldn't go deaf. "Who is she?" she asked. "Is she nice? What does she look like? How serious is it?"

He chuckled and bent to pick up the tennis ball Sarge had dropped at his feet a few seconds ago. The dog whined and then barked. Cole threw the ball, sending Honor and Sarge across the lawn and giving himself a few seconds to talk.

"Her name is Berlin Fuller. Of course she's nice. And…it's getting serious, I suppose."

She sighed, a long, drawn-out sound that conveyed happiness and some exasperation. "Finally. One of my boys is going to get married."

Sarge returned with the ball, and Cole gave him a scrub along the head. "Mom, I didn't say I was engaged."

"Hey, you're the only one with a girlfriend, so you're the closest. Will you get married in Utah?"

"Mom," he said. "I'm taking my Scouts camping next weekend."

A long pause came through the line, and his mom said, "That sounds nice, dear," and Cole bent to throw the ball again, a smile on his face.

Ten minutes later, Berlin appeared through the trees. She wore a pair of denim shorts and a blue tank top, her hair shorter than he'd ever seen it. The blonde had started to grow out again, and she'd obviously been to the salon to get it looking more normal. Not that he'd mentioned anything to her about the odd roots and the way the dark color was all wrong for her.

Cole may be in his first serious relationship, but he wasn't stupid. Her false eyelashes had disappeared over the last week too, and he enjoyed the natural beauty of her so much more than the fabricated stuff. Another thing he planned on taking to the grave with him.

Honor saw her first and sprinted toward her. A lesser woman would've stutter-stepped and stalled, but Berlin kept on coming, even crouching down to receive the German shepherd. Her smile was genuine and beautiful, and Cole paused to watch her interact with his dog.

He suddenly wanted to call his mother back and ask how he would know he was in love. He'd never been in love before, and he had no idea what it felt like. But if it was anything like the warm, oozy feeling spreading through him as he watched his girlfriend, he suspected he might be close.

His heart started thudding in his chest a bit too hard for the level of exertion it took to throw a ball. He picked up the orange object and tossed it again, Sarge's tongue flapping as he went after it. Even Berlin wasn't a good distraction for Sarge, and unless Cole hid the ball, Sarge would never stop.

Berlin stood and approached him, radiant with a new hair color and that azure blouse that made her eyes practically electric.

"Hey." He drew her into a hug and ran his non-throwing hand through her hair. The other one was a bit slobbery, and she'd obviously come straight from the salon. "Your hair looks great."

"Starlee is a miracle worker." Berlin stepped back and fingered the ends of her hair. "She managed to even out the color, and it's still long enough for me to pull back." She bent and picked up the ball this time. She handed it to him with a smile, and he tossed it for Sarge. Honor lay down at Berlin's feet instead of going after something she wouldn't be able to get. Smart dog.

"I wondered if you wanted to come to the family dinner this week." Berlin didn't look at him as she said it, so Cole copied her lead and kept his eyes on Sarge.

"I would love that."

"I haven't been since the retirement party."

"Why not?"

She lifted one shoulder in a shrug, but Cole didn't believe she didn't know. He didn't press her on it though. He hadn't been in many relationships, but he knew better than to act like a cop when it came to personal relationships. At least that was what Jordan had told him.

He slipped one arm around her back. "I thought you were going out with Caitlyn and Scotty tonight."

"I am." She leaned into his chest. "Just stopped by when I saw you and your dogs out here."

He often came to this field on the northeast side of Oxbow Park. It was away from the main thoroughfare, bordering the forest, and closest to his house. "Where are you guys going?"

"Oh, Caitlyn's sister invited us to some concert in Vernal. Her boyfriend's band or something at a comedy club."

"You don't sound overly excited about it."

Berlin shrugged again, and Cole tightened his arm around her waist. "You want to talk about it?"

"Talk about what?"

"Whatever is bothering you." Cole thought he'd learned quite a lot about what to say, and when, and when to keep his questions and thoughts to himself as the weeks passed and his relationship with Berlin grew.

She exhaled and finally turned to face him. "I'm worried that my parents won't like you."

He thought of her mother's bright, piercing eyes the Sunday he'd gone to their house to ask after Berlin. "Why does it matter if they like me?" It wasn't like they'd be living with her parents, though she did seem close with her family.

"I guess it doesn't."

"Why wouldn't they like me?" he pressed. "I'm employed. The Chief of Police, which, I gotta say, is kind of impressive. It takes years to get the qualifications for Chief. I'm smart, I'm strong, I'm honest." He hated that he was bragging about himself, but he honestly didn't understand why they wouldn't like him. "I even go to church now."

She nodded, but her melancholy demeanor remained. Cole had never suffered from poor self-esteem before, but now he felt inadequate in ways he'd never considered.

He drew in a big breath and shoved the ball in his back pocket so Sarge would stop. "What time on Wednesday?"

"Six-thirty." She gave him one last smile, stretched up and gave him a chaste kiss, and said, "I have to go meet my friends. I'll call you later."

Cole watched her go back the way she'd come, and then he clipped the leashes on his dogs and headed home for the rest of the evening.

He woke to the pealing of his phone, and he fumbled for the device, which he kept on his nightstand. Never on silent. The Chief of Police rarely slept deeply.

"Hello?" he answered, still squinting, as much as he could open his eyes. They stung, and he knew he hadn't been asleep long enough.

Nothing came through the line, and he drew the phone back to look at the caller. His pulse spiked and he sat up. "Berlin? Are you all right?"

Scratching and what sounded like a scream came through the line. When she didn't answer, Cole flew into action by pulling on a pair of jeans and the nearest T-shirt. He kept the line open as he hurried out to his cruiser. At the station, he burst through the doors and said to Mason, the cop on duty that night, "I need a trace on this call. Now."

Chapter 11

Berlin laughed at Scotty's joke, noticing the way the man beside her couldn't keep his eyes off her best friend. Caitlyn sat beside her sister, along with four members of the band—the fifth being the one now typing something into Scotty's phone. It had been a great set, and Berlin actually enjoyed herself quite a lot.

She'd tried to picture Cole in this setting, and she couldn't do it. Well, she could, but he'd be scoping out how much the girls at the back table were drinking, and which exits were blocked by people, and the fastest way to get out of the building in case something went down. He'd keep his eyes peeled and barely contribute to the conversation.

Thinking like a cop wasn't a bad thing, except for when Berlin just wanted to have fun. Cole had a different brand of fun, and this night out with her friends was refreshing. It also reminded her how much she enjoyed Cole's company, but in a different way.

Dan scooted closer to her, flipping the ends of her hair. "Remember me?"

A vein of unease squirreled through her, but he didn't touch her again. He had a great smile, sure. And she did remember him, but she'd been hoping he hadn't remembered her, what with the different hair color and the eight years since she'd last seen him.

"Sure." She had to shout to be heard over the din in the comedy club. Another band had set up and they didn't have quite the way with a melody that the men at her table did. She sipped her soda.

"I think you worked at the grocer in Brush Creek for like, a minute." She gave him a smile, hoping it said *we can talk, but I'm not going out with you and don't you dare touch me again.*

Dan returned the smile. "I was there about three weeks, actually."

"Ah, three weeks." She nodded like that was all anyone ever worked at their jobs.

"We got coffee once."

"Yes, we did." Eight years ago. When she was nineteen. She still didn't know the guy's last name.

"Maybe you'd like to do that again." He tapped his fingertips on the tabletop and wouldn't take his eyes off her.

Before Berlin could tell him she was seeing someone else, his hand covered hers and someone barked, "Berlin."

She spun toward the familiar, beastly voice to look up into Cole's face. He wore an expression of anger and relief, which really didn't mix well. "What's going on here?" he growled.

All the conversations at the table ceased, and the lead singer of the band on stage said, "That's it for us. Thanks."

A smattering of clapping lifted into the air, and then it felt like the entire club took a breath and held it.

Berlin tugged her hand out from under Dan's and stood. "What are you doing here?"

"You called me." He held up his phone, where a timer on her call ticked up to fifty-one minutes.

She patted her pockets as Cole glared around the table like everyone there should be arrested for questioning. "I don't even know where my phone is." She wanted to punch Dan when he stepped to her side.

"Is this guy bothering you?"

Cole switched his gaze to Dan, and Berlin was surprised the grocery-store-stock-boy-turned-drummer didn't incinerate on the spot. "Bothering her? You're bothering me, pal."

"Cole." Berlin placed a palm on his chest and pushed. He didn't so much as budge a single centimeter, nor did he look at her. "Outside. Now."

Everyone in the club was watching them now, and she saw how disheveled Cole looked, what with his T-shirt on backward and all.

"Go," she said again, her voice practically echoing off the pipes in the industrial ceiling. "Right now."

He glared at Dan for another moment and said, "She's mine, pal," before leaving.

Berlin's lungs quaked. *She's mine?* What in the world did that mean? The door slammed behind him, and she turned on wooden legs back to her table. "I'm so sorry," she said in a voice that belonged to a rabbit. "Caitlyn, I'll catch a ride back to town with Cole."

She and Scotty stood and enveloped her in a hug. "You sure?" Caitlyn whispered.

"I'll leave right now," Scotty said.

"I can stay with my sister," Caitlyn added.

Berlin thought of how Scotty had been flirting with the bass guitarist, and how happy Caitlyn had been to meet up with her sister. So she held onto them for an extra moment and then cleared her throat. "No, really. You guys stay. I'll be fine." She nodded once, then again, and took a deep, deep breath before she faced the exit.

She marched out with a strong stride that faltered the moment she saw Cole pacing in the parking lot, the red and blue lights of his police vehicle circling. The red-blue red-blue swirls made her a little queasy.

"What was that?" Her tone broadcasted her displeasure, and she took in the car. He'd driven here as if on police business. The call had only been fifty-one minutes old, and it was a solid hour drive from Brush Creek. "How did you even know where I was?"

He stormed toward her. "I traced your phone call."

Her eyebrows flew up as fury filled her. "You traced my call." She'd never be able to go anywhere without him knowing. Flashes of Marc and his insane possessive behavior blinked through her mind's eye.

"You were holding hands with another guy. Who is he, huh?"

Berlin couldn't even imagine what Cole would do if he knew she had gone out with Dan *eight years ago.* "I was not holding hands with him. That guy was just a little touchy-feely. I was handling it."

His laugh sounded anything but happy. "You were handling it. Right." Cole ran his fingers through his hair and looked at her, his hard gaze softening the tiniest bit. "I was worried about you."

"So you drove for an hour just to be the barking beast?" She shook her head, her earlier misgivings about Cole surfacing, and surfacing fast. "You don't *own* me, Cole. I'm not your...your *property*." She folded her arms to keep the trembling dormant though it was a warm night.

"I—"

"And I don't appreciate the jealous boyfriend routine. I've been there, and done that, and I'm not doing it again."

His gray eyes looked like bottomless pits, and he practically spat out the words, "I thought you were in trouble."

"But when you walked in, and clearly saw that I wasn't, why couldn't you just, I don't know." She threw her hands into the air. "Get in your police car and go home." The lights still flashed in her face every other second, and in that moment, she hated them. Hated that he had access to her wherever she went. Hated that he'd made her feel like an object to be bought and sold.

"You should go," she said, trying to be brave and strong and commanding, the way he always was. In reality, her voice trembled and the cop in Cole definitely heard it.

"I should go? Are you going to come with me?"

Deciding on the spot, Berlin said, "No. I came to hang out with my friends tonight." She advanced forward a step. "I told you who I'd be with, and what I'd be doing. I said I'd call when I got home." She poked his chest, causing him to flinch. "You don't get to come barging in because you were worried. That's not a good enough excuse."

She turned around to go back inside, not stopping even when he called, "Berlin," after her.

Pausing with her door on the handle, she half-twisted back to him. "Go home, Cole. And fix your T-shirt. It's on backward." She opened the door and went inside, finally feeling a measure of power in the relationship where he'd always been in the driver's seat.

She returned to the table, taking a spot between Scotty and Caitlyn so she didn't have to deal with Handsy Dan.

"Everything okay?" Caitlyn asked.

"Just fine," she said. "I just didn't want to go with him like I thought I would."

"Did you guys break up?" Scotty whispered.

Berlin didn't want to answer that question. But she said, "Not yet," with a measure of doom in her voice.

———

INSTEAD OF CALLING Cole like she'd said she would, she texted him when she got home. *Made it home safe. Just wanted you to know.*

She feared that if she didn't let him know, he'd be busting down her front door before dawn. She stepped out of her clothes and her shoes before slipping into her pajamas. She collapsed on the bed without taking off her makeup, knowing she'd pay for it in the morning with red, watery eyes until at least noon.

Can we talk? His text made her anger soften, but she really didn't want to speak with him until her head was clear. She'd stayed silent for the ride home, glad Caitlyn and Scotty didn't ask her more questions or pressure her to tell them how she felt.

She didn't know how she felt.

Not right now, she tapped out and sent before silencing her phone.

Before she could set it on the charger, another message from Cole came in. *When?*

She closed her eyes as Brownie hopped up onto the bed beside her. She stroked his soft fur and said,

"Where's Cocoa?" The other Lhasa Apso made an appearance, stepping gingerly over the blankets until she came to Berlin's other side.

"Oh, there she is. Hey, Cocoa. What did you guys do tonight, huh? Huh?" She gave them both a scrub while her phone continued to bleep and flash at her. "I listened to a great band, and talked with my friends. Then Cole came in—you guys remember Cole, right? He has the two big shepherds."

Berlin stared at the ceiling, wishing with everything inside her that she wasn't talking to two dogs right now. She didn't want to come home to four-legged friends, but someone who would listen to her, be her partner, hold and comfort her when she needed it, or celebrate with her when something amazing happened.

For a few weeks now, she'd been picturing Cole in that role. Cole as the one she came home to. Cole who would listen, comfort, talk, and celebrate with her.

But the man she'd seen at the club tonight? She didn't want any part of that man. And maybe that was who Cole really was. A beast.

"Anyway, Cole came in," she continued for Brownie and Cocoa. "And we got in a fight, and I think it's over for us." Tears pricked her eyes and she didn't try to hold them back.

Cocoa whined, almost the more perceptive and sensitive of the two dogs and snuggled her head right up under Berlin's chin.

She already wouldn't be able to sleep tonight, but she

hoped Cole would, so she decided to wait until morning to let him know he didn't need to come to the family dinner on Wednesday, and he didn't need to waste his police resources on her anymore.

She wasn't sure why she'd stopped by the bakery before going to the station. She didn't want to hurt Cole, but she didn't want to be tracked down every time she went to lunch with her mom, or out with her friends, or over to the office to work on a Sunday afternoon.

The clock ticked to seven, and she got out of her car. She'd considered texting him, but in the end, she couldn't do it. He deserved a face-to-face discussion and break up. They'd been seeing each other for over two months, and while big topics like children and marriage hadn't come up yet, Berlin had felt like they were right around the corner.

Cole hadn't arrived yet. She knew because he always parked right out front, and his cruiser wasn't there. The building was unlocked, so she went in, glad most of the desks were empty.

A cop looked up from his station and said, "Berlin. Good morning."

"Hey, Mason. Can I wait in the Chief's office?"

"Yeah, sure." He looked surprised. "You're okay then?"

She stalled in her hasty stride toward Cole's corner office. "Of course I'm okay. Why wouldn't I be?"

"I ran the trace for the Chief last night. He seemed pretty freaked out. Have you talked to him?"

"Yes, we've spoken." She lifted the pink pastry box that held his favorite morning snack—a peach and pecan tart. "I'll just wait in here. Thanks, Mason."

He nodded and she went into Cole's office. It smelled like him, that deep, rich spiciness of his aftershave and the fresh cotton scent of his uniform.

She set the pink box on his desk and stayed standing as she looked at the certifications he'd gotten framed over the years. They sat on a bookshelf and listed the trainings and courses he'd taken. The certificate from the FBI National Academy sat at the top, with beautiful gold lettering, and she reached out to trace his name.

"You have to be nominated to get into that program."

She spun to find him standing in the doorway, tall and impressive in his black uniform. "And then they have to invite you. Can't even apply."

She nodded and moved out of his way so he could step around his desk and sit down. "I brought you a tart," she said.

He didn't open the box or say thank you, almost like he knew why she was there. He probably did.

"I don't think we should see each other anymore." She'd said those exact words several times over the years, but never had it tore through her throat this much. Never had she wanted to recall the words as soon as she'd said them. Never had it felt like she was ripping her heart out and leaving it behind.

Cole didn't blink. "So that's it."

"I think so, yeah."

"So you can make mistakes and apologize and I forgive you, but I don't get the same luxury?"

Berlin didn't want to fight. Didn't have it in her. Not today. "I guess not." She started for the door, guilt gutting her. She expected him to step in front of her, place his big palm against the door so she couldn't get out. Heck, she would've taken him calling after her to please come back.

Instead, the only words she heard were, "Thank you for the tart."

Cole had endured bad days before, but nothing like this Saturday where Berlin had left his office after breaking up with him.

After he'd yelled at Lesli for the third time, she'd gotten in his face and told him to go home until he could treat people kindly. And he had, but being home with Sarge and Honor was no better. At least they knew how to stay out of his way and offer comfort at the same time.

He didn't go to the office on Sunday either. Or church. He simply wanted to stay away from people until he could do what his secretary had told him to do—be kind.

And he simply didn't know how to do that without Berlin in his life.

He knew how to run, so he did that. He knew how to drive around town and look like he was busy, so he did that. He didn't have to worry about running into Berlin, because she was buried with work, between her regular job and the police department audit. She only had a few weeks left to complete that, and her requests for an extension had been denied.

He wasn't sure why the City Council or the City Controller wouldn't grant her more time to complete the audit, but they wouldn't. She'd confessed to him on multiple occasions that she hoped she could finish it in time, and he'd been hanging around her office every Sunday after church since the one where she'd left church early and disappeared.

He hated her disappearance from his life. He'd known it was somewhat empty before, but now his entire existence felt hollow.

He had no drive anymore. No desire to do anything, even so much as throw a ball for Sarge, much to the dog's disappointment.

Pioneer Day in Utah was a state holiday, complete with family barbecues, parades, and fireworks. He put himself on patrol, not only to give the other guys a chance to spend time with their families, but because if he wasn't working, he'd be sitting home feeling sorry for himself.

He directed traffic after the parade and hurried home to feed himself and the dogs before he went to the park to oversee the carnival. Jordan met him in the parking lot with a nod and a fist bump.

As they walked around, casually looking left and

right, it felt very much like the summer fair, which had happened a lifetime ago, to another man.

"So what happened with you and Berlin?" Jordan asked. He was smart and didn't look at Cole when he spoke.

"Things got…too hard." He didn't want to say anything bad about her. The fact that she'd caused him grief by kissing him in front of her family always made him see just a hint of red, but he wouldn't badmouth her to anyone.

"Oh," Jordan said. "I thought you two were a good match. You liked her, didn't you?"

"Yeah." Cole didn't know what else to say. There wasn't anything else. He'd treated her in a way she didn't like, and he didn't know how to fix it. Without her, he felt wild, out of control, and like he might snap at anyone, for any reason, in any moment.

She'd tamed all of that out of him, made him want to be a better man, slow down and think rationally and then speak with kindness and respect.

I tried, he thought, realizing he hadn't told his mother about the break up yet. She'd be devastated, as Cole knew from their weekly talks that none of his brothers were dating anyone yet.

The afternoon wore on, and the large grassy field started to fill with families, couples, food, and coolers as the town of Brush Creek prepared for their fireworks. Cole wasn't sure he could stay and take part in the celebration.

Exhaustion coated his bones from the inside out, and all he could think about was the last time he was in this field. He'd lain on his back to watch the fireworks, Berlin curled into his side, sighing and oohing with the crowd.

He'd put in a fourteen-hour day when he found another pair of officers. "I'm gonna head out," he told Mason and Tate. "Jordan will join you two."

"You're not going to stay for the fireworks?" Tate asked, tilting his head to the side as if he could understand the Chief better that way. He was also Berlin's brother-in-law, and Cole had avoided the man for the past ten days since she'd left him standing in his office with a tart he'd never eaten.

"I'm not much of a fireworks guy," he said.

His officers let him go, and Cole took another circuit around the field alone, trying to find another person, someone, anyone, who was alone the way he was.

They didn't seem to exist in Brush Creek, and for the first time since he'd left home twenty years ago, he felt truly isolated from everyone, almost like a pane of glass had been put between him and them and he hadn't realized it.

"Hey." Tate jogged up to him. "You should stay. Wren's got our daughter and tons of candy. She said you could sit with her."

"Berlin's not with her?" After all, Cole knew Berlin and Wren were close. Not only had he observed it by the way Berlin sat next to Wren every week at church and helped her with her niece, he'd overheard phone conversations between the two of them, knew they worked together in the same office, and listened when Berlin told him that Wren was the best big sister.

Tate shifted and squirmed, which gave Cole his answer as he'd never seen a Marine show any signs of nerves. "I'm not—she broke up with me."

The people closest to him looked up, and a pinch of frustration pulled through him. "I have to go."

Tate got right in his face, the way Cole would expect a Marine to do. "Just answer one question for me, and then you can go."

"Fine." If it would get the guy out of his face, Cole would do it. He respected Tate a lot. He'd brought two dogs to their K9 unit and had been working with them for almost a year. He had patience by the truckload and a vulnerability about him that made the other officers trust him.

"Are you in love with her?" Tate's dark eyes flashed with challenge, and Cole's muscles tightened in response. Fight or flight.

"I—"

"Yes or no," Tate amended. "No I don't knows."

Cole clenched his teeth together. "Maybe."

"Yes or no," Tate pressed.

"I plead the fifth." Cole stepped past Tate and strode out of the park without looking back. He could see the fireworks just fine from his front porch if he so chose. But he didn't want the happy, sparkling bursts of color in his life. Not if he didn't have Berlin to share them with.

How could she sit with Wren and not even think about the last time she'd been in that park, watching fireworks? Was she dying a slow death too? Was every day, every hour, every minute this level of torture for her?

The thought made his chest collapse. He hadn't wanted to hurt her. He hadn't wanted to get hurt. But he supposed that was what happened when a person fell, and he'd definitely fallen in love with Berlin Fuller.

"Yes," he whispered as he climbed his front steps and shut himself behind the very solid front door. "The answer to your question, Officer Benson, is yes."

He didn't want to own her. He simply wasn't complete without her, and she should know that before too much time went by.

And now that Cole had admitted to himself that he loved Berlin, he needed to do something to get her back in his life.

CHAPTER 13

Berlin read over the police department audit one last time, just to make sure every I was dotted and every T crossed. She checked page breaks and insertions and merge codes. If she looked at it any longer, she might just select all the text and push delete.

So she saved the document and sent five copies to the printer. One for the City Controller. One for the City Council. One for the mayor. One for public record. One for the Chief of Police.

Ah, the Chief.

He was never far from her thoughts, but she refused to let herself dwell on him for longer than seven seconds. She'd read somewhere that if thoughts could be redirected before giving them too much attention, they could be reformed. She desperately didn't want Cole to plague her. At one point, she'd planned to live in Brush

Creek indefinitely with him and that horrible first date at the crepery.

She could do it again. Their circles really had no reason to cross, other than this audit.

"Which is now finished." She collated the reports and put them together into little booklets. She hated this secretarial work when she knew how she'd neglected her regular job. Wren had assured her it was fine, that they could wait to get their accounts payable and receivable sorted out, but Berlin hated the backlog of work when everything wasn't done on a monthly basis.

She put the anxiety to the side and left the offices in favor of the city buildings a couple of blocks away. She hand-delivered all the audit reports until she only had one left. She didn't have to hand it directly to Cole. No, her plan was to give it to Lesli, his secretary.

Then, onto lunch, she thought. She and Caitlyn had taken a half-day off of work so they could get together over salads and sodas.

Berlin had spoken to no one about her break up with Cole. Wren knew, of course, but she didn't question Berlin at the office, through texts, nothing. She really was the best big sister a girl could hope for.

In a town the size of Brush Creek, everyone knew the Chief was back on the market anyway. Berlin didn't need to explicitly say anything to anyone, and she'd already asked Caitlyn to keep Cole out of their lunch conversation. Her friend had agreed.

She eyed the cruiser that she'd ridden in dozens of

times as she approached the station. Cole was inside. It had been just over two weeks since she'd ended their relationship, and she wanted to run and hide for another year.

"You'll have to see him sometime," she whispered to the stuffy, late-summer atmosphere. So she pulled in a lungful of that suffocating air and entered the police station.

Activity hummed like a well-oiled machine, and a few officers glanced up and acknowledged her. She went straight to Lesli's desk and asked, "Is the Chief in?"

Lesli, who seemed to know everything before it happened, actually looked away from her paperwork. "Berlin. How are you, dear?" She got up and came around her desk to hug Berlin, not something that was terribly uncommon.

"Fine." Berlin laughed lightly. "Just fine, Lesli. How are you?"

"Oh, I'd be better if that monster of a Chief didn't sit and bark at people all day."

Berlin's gaze switched to the doorway behind Lesli's desk. "Is today a good day or a bad day?"

"Oh, honey, since you two broke up, every day has been a bad day." Lesli gave her a sympathetic smile and sat back down. "I can take that, if you'd like."

Berlin hugged the inch-thick report to her chest. "I can give it to him." She glanced over Lesli's head to the rectangular doorway. The blinds were closed but the door open. Cole had to be in there, but she couldn't see him yet.

Employing her bravery, she stepped around Lesli's desk and toward Cole's office, a few short strides getting her to the doorway. She knocked on the frame. "I have the financial audit complete."

He looked up and their eyes locked. She threw the bound report out in front of her like a shield. "I think you passed."

Cole stood, a storm raging in his expression. She couldn't decide if he was happy to see her or not. Probably not. He hadn't tried calling or texting her once. He'd never checked in about the audit.

She glanced toward the back corner and found a cot sitting there, a blanket folded on top of it. Surprise bolted through her, along with a bit of sadness. He slept here? Why was he sleeping here? He'd never mentioned that to her, and she wondered if the late summer and early fall festivities had kept him so busy he couldn't even walk a couple of blocks to go home.

He moved in front of the makeshift bed and reached for the report. She gave it to him, their fingers touching the booklet at the same time for only a moment. Too long and too short at the same time.

"Thank you," he said without looking at the audit. "I can't believe you got it done on time."

"Well, Paul wouldn't give me an extension, so." Berlin rocked back on her heels and gave him a smile that felt strained. "Well, I'll see you later." She turned, her first step putting her back in the main room, away from the scent of his cologne and the gorgeous sight of his face.

She may have imagined it, but she thought she heard him call her name. She kept going, sure she could cite the din in the police station as a reason for why she hadn't turned back.

Her pulse felt like the beating of hummingbird wings by the time she reached the exit. She ducked to the side and pressed her back into the hot brick, trying to get a cleansing breath. She'd done it. She'd talked to him and not thrown herself into his arms. Seen him, and he looked good. Maybe he wasn't getting enough sleep—and that cot in the corner of his office concerned her—but that was normal. Even hearing that he was acting like a monster brought her some level of relief.

Cole was acting like he always had, so their break up must not have damaged him too badly. Berlin wasn't sure if she should be happy about that or not. As she got in her car to go to lunch with Caitlyn, her heart wailed. It definitely wasn't happy that Cole didn't seem to care that they weren't together anymore.

RUBY'S ROOST at lunchtime was like a carnival. People laughed and chatted, the scent of delicious frying food filled the air, and the whole place was packed with locals. Everyone from the pastor and his wife, to construction workers, to moms getting together for a couple of hours, to a handful of businessmen.

Berlin slid into the booth where Caitlyn waited and said, "You've got blue paint by your right eyebrow."

Caitlyn reached up and touched the offending brow and smiled. "Finger painting today at the preschool."

"Of course." Berlin didn't need a menu, so when the waitress came, she ordered a plate of French fries, a big Caesar salad, and a round of pork potstickers. Not exactly a trio of foods that went together, but exactly what she wanted.

Caitlyn didn't bat an eye as she put in an equally odd order of cream of broccoli soup, a plate of chicken fettuccini, and two cups of Diet Coke. "Those kids really keep me drinking the stuff," she said with a shrug. "I already have a headache because I haven't had as much today as I usually do."

"You're a saint," Berlin said. "How's Robert?"

"Oh, so we can talk about my boyfriend but not yours?"

Berlin leveled her gaze at Caitlyn. "I don't have a boyfriend." But she did want to talk about him, just for a moment. "I saw him today. Ten minutes ago, in fact."

Caitlyn leaned in, her eyes positively dancing. "You did? Did he finally show up at the office with flowers and cake and a live band to serenade you?"

Berlin couldn't help the smile that touched her lips. "No. And now no matter what I say, it will sound stupid."

Caitlyn laughed and reached for the Diet Coke the waitress put in front of her. She unwrapped two straws and put one in each cup before drinking, drinking, drinking. She smacked her lips and gave a very loud sigh.

Berlin shook her head and put a straw in her own soda. "I took him the police audit. We spoke for a minute or two. I survived."

"Mm hm." Caitlyn glanced up when the soup came. She opened a package of crackers and broke them into the soup. "I don't know if I should say this or not, but let the record show that you brought up Cole."

Berlin leaned into her arms on the table. "All right. Say it."

"Honey, you are so far from surviving, it's not even funny. I don't even know what to call it. It's the *opposite* of surviving."

"Whatever." Berlin looked away, out across the busy restaurant. "I'm still alive. I go to work. I even made dinner last week. That's the very definition of survival."

Caitlyn shook her head, but she wasn't upset or frustrated. "You'll get back together with him."

"I don't think so, Cait." She could still see the absolute rage in his eyes as he stood in the comedy club. Though he'd spoken pretty words about being concerned about her, he'd allowed his jealousy to take over. And she didn't need that every time she left the house.

"Has he called at all?"

"Not even once." Berlin heard the misery in her

voice, and she hated it. "Okay, no more talk about Cole. I really did want to know how Robert was doing."

"He'll keep." Caitlyn took her time to take another bite of soup and then a long draw of her soda. "Just answer one more question. Don't think about it. Just answer. Okay?"

The conversation paused while the waitress arrived with another woman, both of them carrying a few plates. The French fries, the salad, the potstickers, and Caitlyn's pasta got placed and moved and arranged.

Berlin picked up her fork, intending to eat the salad first, as the waitresses moved away.

"You ready?" Caitlyn mixed her pasta and sauce, her eyes expectant.

"I'm ready."

"No thinking."

"Caitlyn."

"Just answer."

Berlin rolled her eyes and speared a cucumber. She had it halfway to her mouth when Caitlyn asked, "Are you in love with him?"

An answer sprang to Berlin's mind, but she couldn't get herself to say it.

"You don't have to answer. But think about this: If you are, what are you going to do about it?"

———

LATER THAT NIGHT, Berlin sat on the cement pad in her back yard, watching Brownie and Cocoa romp through the overly long grass. She should get one of her brothers to come clip it for her.

Anything to get Caitlyn's questions out of her head.

Are you in love with him?

Yes.

Yes had popped into Berlin's mind. She'd had enough other relationships to know this one with Cole was different. Had been since the first date. A smile curved her lips as she thought about those disastrous crepes, the horrible silence between them in the car. But their second "first date" had been so much better, and he had taken her heart one piece of a time until he owned it completely.

No wonder she wasn't surviving. After all, a person couldn't really live without their most vital organ.

What are you going to do about it?

Caitlyn's second question really plagued Berlin, even as she made the call to Kyler about her yard, and as she fed her dogs, and as she put on a crime drama at a volume that was almost painful.

"I have to do something," she said, the loud car chase on the screen in front of her swallowing the sound of her words.

What could she do?

Forgive.

Just like at the restaurant, the answer was simply there. Berlin seized onto it, but fumbled with how to *do* it. Pastor Peters made it sound so easy in his Sunday morning sermons.

Berlin pushed a button and turned off the television. Instantly her thoughts quieted too. She half-expected a rush of forgiveness to flood her, though she knew it didn't quite work that way.

"How do I forgive him, Lord?" she asked, her voice on the outer edge of pain. No immediate answer came.

CHAPTER 14

Seeing Berlin—talking to her—was an exquisite kind of torture Cole never wanted to experience again. At the same time, the desire to see her again had him falling to his knees right there beside the cot in his office.

Only the two night cops remained in the station, and they knew not to bother him unless it was an emergency.

He'd been searching for a while to get Berlin back into his life, and he couldn't think of a single thing short of loading up his dogs and going over to his house. He imagined himself knocking nicely, hanging his head, and apologizing over and over until she forgave him.

He didn't take flowers. He didn't ask her to meet him somewhere. Berlin wouldn't do that anyway.

He finished his prayer, utterly spent. He worked out in the morning and the evening now, really putting the treadmills in the gym in the basement of the station through long sessions. Completely exhausting himself was the only way he got any sleep at all.

He hadn't even looked at the audit she'd brought by a few days ago. He was sure it was one hundred percent accurate. Everything Berlin did in her professional life was flawless. She might have made a few mistakes with Cole, but he had too. The biggest one.

He settled onto the cot, the narrowness of it a jab to his broad shoulders. But he couldn't go home. For some reason, he felt too lonely there.

Sarge jumped up onto the cot like it was big enough for him. "Lay down," Cole said while the dog tentatively searched for somewhere he could be comfortable. Honor didn't try getting on the cot. Instead she circled on the floor near Cole's head and he scrubbed behind her ears after she settled down.

The dogs had spent lots of time at the station, both during the day and at night, so Cole didn't feel too bad about their sleeping conditions.

In the morning, he ordered flowers to be delivered to Berlin's home. He hadn't contacted her or sent anything since they'd broken up, but now that he'd seen her and talked to her, however briefly, the time felt right.

Hours later, his phone buzzed, and he almost fell out of his chair when he saw Berlin's name on his screen. *Thank you for the flowers.*

Cole stood, his heart hammering, sending vibrations through his whole body. He knew where she was, and he didn't think twice before grabbing his keys and heading for the exit. He ignored everyone who tried to grab him for just a quick second, only pausing to hold the door open for Sarge and Honor.

He drove rationally, at least until he turned onto Berlin's street. Her car sat in the driveway, and he pulled behind it at an angle so she couldn't get out. He flipped on the lights on top of his car and said, "All right, guys. It's now or never. Should we go see if she'll talk to us?"

Sarge whined, and Cole felt the same way. Anxious. Jittery. Unsure.

He got out of the cruiser anyway, letting the dogs follow him out the driver's door though he normally made them wait for him to open one of the back doors. His steps slowed the closer to the front door he got, and he stopped completely when Berlin opened the door and filled the frame.

"Berlin," he said, his voice a little more beastly than he liked. He tried to soften it, but several feet still separated them, and his dogs had started barking at the sight of her two pups. She bent down and acknowledged the German shepherds before going back into her house, taking all four canines with her.

She hadn't said anything. Not a single word, and Cole wasn't sure if he should go inside or wait right where he was. He climbed the steps but paused short of entering her home. Her private space.

The red and blue lights rotated, splashing color into her living room—and across her face as she turned from the back door. "What are you doing here, Cole?"

Oh, she couldn't say his name. That tore a hole right through his chest, and he stepped through the door, a speech coming into his mind.

"I'm in love with you." He cleared his throat so he didn't sound so growly. "You've stolen my heart, and I need to take you down to the station to ask a few questions."

She leaned against the back of the couch and folded her arms. "A few questions?"

"Yes, ma'am. It'll only take a few minutes. I'm sure the dogs will be fine." He was not going to be fine if he couldn't make things right with her.

"Ask them here."

Cole couldn't seem to find a comfortable position with which to stand. "All right. Do you intend to stay mad at me forever?"

She blinked, her eyes lovely and intense as they watched him. "No."

Hope ballooned inside his chest. "Did you hear me say I'm in love with you?" The order of his questions was all skewed, but he didn't exactly have a script.

"I did."

"And?"

"And what?"

"I'm so sorry, Berlin." His emotions caught on her name. "I don't think I own you. There's no way anyone on this earth could own you. You're smart, and driven, and beautiful, and I know you don't need me." He took a step closer, his throat so, so dry. "But I need you. I'm dying a little more each day without you."

She straightened, opened her mouth, and promptly shut it again.

Encouraged that she hadn't thrown him out yet, he inched forward again. "Tell me what to do," he begged. "And I will do it."

She sighed and shook her head. "You don't need to do anything."

"Obviously, I do. Please." He wanted to fall to his knees and beg, but he didn't. "Please forgive me."

Berlin gazed up at him, warring emotions streaming through her expression. She never was great at hiding how she felt, and Cole wanted to keep talking but he'd run out of things to say.

"Have you had lunch?" she asked.

"No."

"Want to take me to lunch?"

"When did you start to ask the questions?" He smiled, his hope soaring when she returned the gesture.

"Want to get over here and kiss me? Make me stop with all the questions?"

Cole didn't need to think twice about that. He swept her into his arms, murmured, "I'm so sorry," one more time, and then kissed her like he loved her—because he did.

She pulled away earlier than he would've liked, given that he hadn't held her or kissed her in what felt like a lifetime. His love blossomed, and bloomed, and swelled as they breathed together.

And when she said, "I love you too, Cole," in the softest, sweetest voice, his life was indeed, complete.

"Do you think the third time will be the charm?" She pressed her forehead against his collarbone and swayed with him.

"The third time?" He ran his hands up and down her back, completely mesmerized by the smell of her, the taste, the feel of her body beside his.

"Our third first date."

A chuckle started deep in his gut and grew, expanding until it filled his whole chest, his whole soul, and her whole house. He sobered and looked into her eyes. "I sure hope so, sweetheart. I can't lose you again."

"You're not a bad catch yourself." She tipped up on her toes and kissed him again. He liked what she'd said, but she'd gotten it all wrong. He wasn't the good catch here. She was, and he needed to do everything in his power to make sure she didn't get away from him again.

BERLIN KEPT Cole to herself for another month. Then two. When he pulled up to her house to take her to dinner on her birthday, the evidence that her family had been there overwhelmed him. At least two dozen balloons billowed in the autumn breeze, though their colorful strings kept them tied to the porch railings.

He hit a baby blue one out of his way as he mounted the steps. Her front door had been covered in long sheets of yellow paper and a huge number 28 had been painted in bright purple. So he was officially not a decade older than her anymore, and that felt mighty nice as he rapped on the door.

"Come in!" she called, her voice with a fringe of franticness in it.

He opened the door and went in, the scent of chocolate and cream obvious in the air. So she'd already celebrated, and that didn't settle well in his gut. He caught a flash of her as she darted down the hall.

"I'll be right back," she called.

Cole had spent many hours on her couch, holding her, talking, and falling asleep to the sound of a movie they'd put on. He sat down there again, trying not to feel too depressed about being the last one to wish her happy birthday.

With the Halloween children's parade and the town trick-or-treat festival coming up, it had been all hands on deck at the station. They'd had the County Sheriff's department in town for trainings, and Cole had spent long hours at work recently.

Including today. He'd given two assignments away so he could be at Berlin's at a decent hour—and it was still too late.

Her heels clicked behind him, and he stood to receive her. She wore a beautiful, form-fitting black dress with sleeves that went just below her elbow. He whistled as he scanned her. "Aren't you a sight for sore eyes?"

A grin graced her face, and he thought she looked older. More mature. Or maybe he just hadn't seen her for a few days. Her hair had grown back out to its normal color, and he liked the blonde locks much better than the dark.

Her penetrating blue eyes drank him up as well, and he realized she was gripping something in her hand. "What's that?" he asked.

Silently, she extended her hand to reveal a black velvet ring box. Cole's pulse rioted and he locked his eyes on hers, unsure of what to say. No way she was proposing to him. *No way.*

"I don't really know what you got me for my birthday," she started.

"Berlin," he interrupted, his tone a bit on the beastly side. "Please don't do this."

"Do what?"

"*I* want to ask you." The last couple of months had been some of the happiest of his life. He'd thought long and hard about how to propose to Berlin, and while he wasn't much for grand gestures and huge, romantic affairs, he thought he could do a decent job of buying a ring and getting down on one knee. But not if she asked him first.

"Ask me what?" She tilted her head as if she really didn't know.

"To marry me," he said bluntly. "*I* want to ask *you* to marry *me.*"

The surprise wasn't hard to find in her eyes. Nor the panic. "Oh."

Confusion filled him too. "Are you—what *is* that?"

She cracked the lid of the box and said, "It's a ring for my mother. Her birthday is next week, and I thought it would be a great time for you to finally come meet my family."

He stared at the silver ring with the green gem in it, still reeling. "So...you bought me a gift to give her?"

"Something like that."

"What does this have to do with your birthday?"

She shrugged and took a tentative step closer, her face open and vulnerable now. "I was just going to say that I didn't know what you'd gotten me, but that all I really want is for you to be part of my family." She ducked her head, her hair falling over her shoulder.

Cole moved forward and pushed it back. "That's all I want too."

She looked up at him and let the ring box drop to her side. He encircled her in an embrace as she said, "So you're going to ask me to marry you?"

"Well, not today." He forced a laugh out of his throat. "But yeah. I mean...yeah."

"When?" she pressed.

"I don't know." Honestly, he'd been waiting to meet her family. He told her that, and she said, "So I guess we're on the same page then."

"Close to it," he said, stepping back and taking the ring from her. "Is this an emerald?"

"Yep. My mother loves emeralds."

"So we'll go to the family dinner next week."

"Six-thirty." At least she didn't look as unsure this time as she had the last time she'd invited him to come.

"You sure you want to go out tonight?" he asked, his self-consciousness rearing its ugly head.

"Why wouldn't I?"

"You've already had a celebration." He glanced around her house. "Several, it looks like."

Her gaze was filled with fire and passion when she said, "You're the only one I want to see on my birthday. Of course I want to go to dinner."

Cole smiled and swept one arm around her waist. "And you want to dance."

She laughed and hugged him tight. "Yes, I want to dance. And I want some of that chocolate tuxedo cake for my birthday." She sobered and looked at him. "And you. I want you."

I want you wasn't quite the same as *I love you*, but it made Cole's blood burn through his body just as hot.

"I want you too," he whispered just before kissing her. "Happy birthday, sweetheart."

CHAPTER 15

Berlin paced on her front porch, her eyes stuck to the road in front of her house. Cole was late. He was hardly ever late, though his job did keep him past when he said he'd be done from time to time. It was something she'd gotten used to, but her family wouldn't like it.

Six-thirty had come and gone ten minutes ago, and he'd texted two minutes ago to say he was on his way. Sure enough, he came around the corner on her next breath, and she flew down the front steps to meet him at the curb.

"Sorry," he said when she opened the door. "I got hung up."

"It's okay." The five-minute drive wouldn't kill them. Her mom had said they'd hold dinner until Cole and Berlin arrived. So why did Berlin feel like she'd swallowed jumping beans?

Everyone knew about her and Cole, about the break up over the summer, the bad first date, all of it. They'd actually met him before. But this family dinner felt bigger and more important than her father's retirement party, where the whole town had been invited.

Cole pulled past the house and parked on the street before turning to face her. "Okay? You have the ring?"

"Yes." Berlin opened her purse and handed it to him. She'd wrapped a white ribbon around the ring box and added a tiny card that she'd made during work that day.

"Let's do this then." Cole exhaled and got out of the car still wearing his uniform, complete with his police utility belt and gun. He really was one of the sexiest men Berlin had ever met, and she couldn't believe he was interested in her.

Stop it, she told herself. She deserved a man as wonderful and strong as Cole, even if he did have a beastly streak sometimes. He'd softened considerably since she'd first met him, and even more since they'd gotten back together.

They didn't go back to the front door and through the house, but simply walked around the side of it and into the back yard. The big picnic table stretched before them, but the children were still playing out in the yard and on the swing set. Most of the adults had congregated in the outdoor kitchen, and Berlin could tell immediately that something was...off.

"Something's going on," she said. "Maybe Fabi or Jazzy is pregnant."

"How can you tell?" Cole threaded his fingers through hers and looked toward the house.

"I just can. Like, why are Wren and Dawn standing like that, with their backs to—?"

Someone must have said something, because the low chatter coming from the outdoor kitchen quieted, and every single person turned and looked at her and Cole. Something was definitely going on, and Berlin's stomach flipped.

Fabi stepped between the crowd of people, with one hand hidden behind her back. She approached Berlin and presented her with a single red rose. Without looking at Cole for even a fraction of a second, she said, "He is in love with you."

As quickly as she'd come, she turned and left. Berlin held the rose by the slender stem, wondering what kind of Fuller family prank this was.

"Come on," Cole said gently, nudging her forward. She'd only taken one step before she realized each of her siblings and their spouses had made a long, single-file line that led to the outdoor kitchen.

Each held a hand behind their back, and as she stepped to Tate, he presented her with another rose and the words, "He's a good boss. A great Chief."

Berlin took the rose and looked at Cole. "You did this."

"I have no idea what you're talking about." He nodded toward Dawn, the next person in line. "But I think she wants to tell you something."

One by one, Berlin accepted roses from her siblings and sibling-in-laws, each with a statement about Cole or something he'd said about her. Her mom and dad were last in line, and her mother's eyes shone with unshed tears as she gave Berlin the last rose and said, "He is the one for you, Berlin."

Berlin could hardly keep her own tears dormant as she hugged her mom. She turned to find Cole, but he'd moved during the embrace.

He cleared his throat, and she spun around to find him down on one knee, a different velvet box held out in front of him.

"I don't think I'm all those things they said," he started. "But I do know I love you, and I will try my best to be the man and husband you deserve." He swallowed, like this speech was hard for him, but he delivered the words with unflinching power, his voice smooth and deep and wonderful, as always.

"Berlin Fuller, will you marry me?"

Gazing down at him, with an armful of red roses with all of their petals, Berlin realized she'd gotten a prince in every sense of the word. She let her tears fall then, which only made the diamond blurry.

"Yes," she said. "Yes, I'll marry you."

He whooped, stood up, and slid the ring on her finger. He kissed her a moment later, wiping her tears with his thumbs as he cradled her face. "I love you so much," he murmured before turning to say, "She said yes!" as if everyone in the yard didn't already know.

All the adults started clapping, and Berlin had to go back down the line to hug her sisters and show them the ring. Berlin had to give her mom credit for letting dinner be postponed even further. She did finally say, "All right. Time to eat," and Berlin returned to Cole's side—where she always wanted to be.

———

BERLIN TWISTED AND TURNED, trying to find the best angle to see the back of the dress.

"Is it on?" Wren asked from the other side of the door. "Come on, we're dying to see it."

Of course, Berlin couldn't go wedding dress shopping by herself. Oh, no. Eight women waited on the other side of the door, and Berlin just wanted a few seconds with herself before she walked out. Because then she'd have to hear eight different opinions and try to judge eight separate reactions.

"Just a second," she called to her sister. Wren would like this dress. Jazzy would pretend to like it. Fabi would say it needed more lace. Her mother would hang back and wait, her expression neutral. Then she'd say something to point out the obvious flaws in the design.

Her mom wanted Berlin to have her grandmother make her dress. Granny Ebony had made a few of the girls' dresses, but Berlin had seen her age, and she didn't want to tax the older woman. So she'd insisted on buying something instead.

She opened the door and said, "I don't know. It feels too plain."

Wren sucked in a breath and put her hand over her heart like this was the only dress Berlin could be married in. "It's not too plain. It's perfect."

"Needs lace," Fabi said while Jazzy did a double and then triple scan of the gown.

Dawn smiled and said, "It is a little plain, but if you like it, it's fine." She was starting to become Berlin's favorite, and she gave Dawn a grateful smile in return.

Scotty and Caitlyn stood behind the row of sisters, and Berlin could tell from their expressions that the dress was okay. Caitlyn even said, "It's okay."

The attendant approached with another dress, this one much lacier and adorned with sparkly beads. Fabi's whole face lit up when she saw it, and Berlin allowed her mom to tug on the sleeves of the plainer gown while Granny Ebony just grinned from her spot in the chair by the entrance to the dressing room.

"We could sew a panel in the back, if that's what you don't like," her mom said.

"I don't know what I don't like," Berlin said. She'd always been told that she'd know "the one true wedding gown" once she put it on, but it hadn't happened yet. They'd been out shopping for three weekends in a row leading up to Christmas, and her mother was nearing the end of her patience for the whole dress shopping experience.

"If you want to get married in March, you better find

a dress quick," was what she'd said when Berlin had sat down with her to put a date on the calendar. She and Cole had thought a short engagement would be best, and March was a good month for him, with few festivals and events he had to coordinate.

So though he'd only asked her to marry him three and a half weeks ago, Berlin felt like if she didn't find a dress today, she'd have to move the wedding back. And she really didn't want to do that.

She put on the fancier dress with the help of the attendant, but it wasn't the one either. "Maybe something halfway between these two," she said, gesturing from the gobs of lace and itchy beads to the plainer A-line dress she'd just had on.

"I'll help her find something," Dawn offered as the attendant handed the two dresses to a second woman and started for the long row of gowns again.

Berlin stood there in a slip, twisting the diamond on her finger, praying with everything she had. She peeked out the door to find only Scotty and Caitlyn still waiting. "Where'd everyone else go?"

"Oh, they all want to pick a dress for you to try on." Caitlyn gave her a smile. "You okay? You look worried."

"I need to find a dress."

Caitlyn gave her a big hug. "And you will. This is the best shop in the county." They'd traveled outside of Brush Creek, and even past Vernal, to a bigger town called Duchesne.

Seemingly as one, her sisters and mother returned, each of them towing a dress with them.

"Mine first," Wren said, her face harboring a happy glow that had nothing to do with her new baby. Two attendants came into the large dressing room with Berlin, and she went through Wren's dress—which she liked okay—Fabi's, and Jazzy's. None of them were exactly right.

Dawn went next, and as the fabric went over Berlin's hips and she put her arms through the straps, she inhaled slowly.

"Yes," the attendant said. "This one's very nice."

Very nice was an understatement. With a lace appliqué across the bodice and then in linear patterns down the front of the dress, it wasn't too much frilly stuff. It felt chic in the A-line design, with a deep V-neckline and wide straps over her shoulders that made her feel feminine and covered though she really wasn't either of those things.

The second attendant zipped the dress and said, "It has a hand-cut box in the back, for just a touch of drama." She finished tying it and Berlin twisted, turned, the sheer panels that ran from the straps to her waist and the box pure perfection. Without warning, she almost started crying.

"Inverted pleats and fully lined," the first woman said. "It's the perfect combination of modern and classic in pure white." She brushed her hand over Berlin's hip, but the dress barely needed to be altered.

"It's perfect, right?" Berlin didn't dare speak too loud, not wanting to jinx anything.

"Let's see what they say." The first woman smiled and opened the door. "Vera Wang," she said.

Berlin stepped out, the long dress pooling at her feet. She felt like a princess in the dress, and she beamed at her family and friends. A hush fell over them, and not even her mother had anything to say.

"It's the one," Berlin declared, finding Dawn's eyes and stepping over to give her very pregnant sister a big hug. "Thank you, Dawn."

There was more spinning, and touching, and oohing, and in the end, Berlin bought the dress and would have it fully altered and ready for her wedding in just three weeks.

Now, if only the wedding would come that fast.

Chapter 16

Cole told his dogs to sit so he could put bow ties on them. Honor got a bright pink, lacy bow that still looked feminine, and Sarge a black, silk one like Cole's. They both seemed to know that they needed to be on their best behavior today.

"I'm getting married," he told them. "So you just get to sit and watch, okay?"

Several of the Fullers had been married in the big family back yard by the river, but in March, there could still be snow on the ground, so he and Berlin had opted for an indoor wedding and reception center.

They partnered with Teddy's, so there would be pulled pork sandwiches, that flavored lemonade he'd fallen in love with, and individual desserts. Berlin had invited him along on as many of the wedding preparations as he could attend, and his favorites had been the food tastings.

The reception center was decked out in Christmas lights and these little puffy flowers that were fake but looked like snowballs. Berlin had picked everything white, yellow, and navy blue, and he'd let her do what she wanted. The cake had a cop on top, with his bride, and Cole had smiled the biggest at that.

The door to the groom's room opened, and his brothers entered, suit bags slung over their shoulders. Cole's smile stayed at the sight of them all gathered in this tiny Utah town for the first Fairbanks wedding.

"You ready for this?" Mathias, the oldest, asked.

"So ready." Cole gave him a hearty pat on the back. "Thanks for coming. I know it wasn't easy."

"Wouldn't miss it."

The other brothers had said similar things, and as soon as their father came in, they all started getting changed, properly tied up, and ready for the nuptials.

Berlin had hired a wedding planner, and the woman wore a headset and barked orders—exactly the kind of control Cole liked. So he knew when he had ten minutes to be on the floor, and that his mother had made it into the bride's room to give Berlin the something borrowed she needed for the ceremony.

The easy time with his family had slipped through Cole's fingers like water. Though they'd been in town for a week, he felt like they'd just arrived. He and Berlin would be leaving for a honeymoon in tropical Cancun the following morning, and as the intercom went off with, "I'm coming to get you now, Chief. Thirty seconds," from the wedding planner, Cole put one arm around his dad and one around his closest brother.

They all got in a circle, and Cole looked at each of them. "Let's get together more often," he said, his voice a little thick. "And maybe not wait for the next wedding, since none of y'all even have girlfriends."

"Hey," Mathias protested. "I'm seeing someone."

"Sure." Cole smiled at him. "But seriously."

Murmurs of assent went around the circle, and then a sharp knock sounded on the door. "I have to go," he said. "Don't want to make Alicia mad."

He opened the door and spread his arms wide. "How'd I do?"

She half-glared, half-scanned him, a tight smile pinching the corners of her mouth. "You look hand-some," she said in an even voice. "Come with me." She pivoted on her toe and marched him down the hall and through a door that led directly to the alter at the front of the room.

The ceremony room looked a lot like a church, but the space didn't have permanent, long benches like the chapel, but individual chairs that came in different colors. Berlin had chosen dark blue with white and yellow bows tied around the backs.

False tree branches extended down from the ceiling, with tea lights and flowers in the colors of the bows. It looked like a magical place to get married, and Cole hoped it was everything Berlin wanted. Because he wanted to give her everything she wanted, always.

The chairs started filling as he got instructions from Pastor Peters. Alicia appeared in the doorway in the back, signaling to find out if everything was set inside. Cole had no idea, so he looked at the preacher.

Pastor Peters gave Alicia a thumbs up, and she backed out of the room. Cole's heart started thumping in his chest like a big, tribal drum. Berlin was going to come through that door any second. His girlfriend. His fiancée. The love of his life, soon to be his wife.

He licked his lips and swallowed, trying to school his emotions. The seconds ticked by, and he thought she'd never come. Maybe she'd left. That really got his pulse accelerated, and he shoved the thoughts away. Berlin had shown no indication that she'd get cold feet.

Sure enough, the door opened only a moment later, and the wedding party started down the aisle. Her nieces were flower girls, throwing white petals as they went. People stood and smiled, but all Cole could do was search for Berlin.

She finally appeared, her dress the most magnificent thing he'd ever seen. It hugged her curves and left her shoulders bare, making his breath catch somewhere in his lungs he didn't think possible.

She held onto her father's arm but she never once looked away from Cole as she trekked toward him. Cole knew then, as he had for months, that he was one of the luckiest men on earth.

Her father passed her to him with a whispered, "She's all yours now, Chief," and she switched her arm to his.

Cole could hardly contain himself, and he suddenly understood why she'd kissed him the way she had at her father's graduation party. Sometimes it couldn't be helped. He leaned down and swept his lips along her right eyebrow instead of bending her backward and really kissing her the way he wanted to.

They faced the pastor, and the ceremony began. It honestly became a blur to Cole. All he could smell was Berlin's fruity, flowery perfume. He could only feel the weight of her hand on his arm.

So when Pastor Peters prompted him to say yes, he did. She said it too. And then the kissing part came, and Cole did exactly what he'd been thinking about: He bent her back and leaned over her as she laughed.

"I love you," he said just before kissing her like the man in love that he was.

Read on for a sneak peek at Book 1 in the Christmas in Coral Canyon Romance series, **GRAHAM!**

G raham Whittaker gazed at the Tetons, wishing just the tops of the mountains were snow-covered. Unfortunately, it hadn't stopped snowing for a few days, and the white stuff covered everything from the mountaintops to the grass outside the lodge he'd just bought and moved into over Christmas.

He liked to think heaven was weeping for the loss of his father, the same way the Whittaker family had been for the past nine days. With the funeral and burial two days past now, everyone had gone back to their normal lives—except Graham.

"This is your normal life now," he told himself as he turned away from what some probably considered a picturesque view of the country, the snow, the mountains.

Whiskey Mountain Lodge was a beautiful spot,

nestled right up against the mountains on the west and the Teton National park on the north. It had a dozen guest rooms and boasted all the amenities needed to keep them fed, entertained, and happy for days on end.

Not that it mattered. Graham wasn't planning on running the lodge as the quaint bed and breakfast in the mountains that it had previously been.

No, Whiskey Mountain Lodge was his new home.

His father had left behind an entire business that needed running, and Graham had nothing left for him in Seattle anyway. So he'd come to help his mother after the sudden death of her husband, and he'd had enough time to find somewhere to live and operate Springside Energy Operations as the CEO.

It was a step up, really. He'd only been the lead developer at Qualetics Robotics in Seattle, but the itch to develop technology and robotics to make people's lives easier had died when his father had.

Graham hoped it would come back; Springside could definitely benefit from having the first fracking robot to identify the natural gases under the surface of the Earth *before* they drilled. But they were years away from that.

Just like Graham felt years away from anyone else out here.

A dog barked, reminding him that he'd inherited his father's dog as well as his company, and he went over to the back door to let Bear back in. The big black lab seemed to move quite slowly, though he still wore his usual smile on his face.

"Hey, Bear." He scrubbed the dog to wipe off the snowflakes that had settled on his back. "Guess I better go check on the horses."

Whiskey Mountain had come with a riding stable, something tourists apparently liked to do in the summer months in Wyoming. Graham had grown up in Coral Canyon, Wyoming, but his parents lived in town, in a normal house, without any horses.

Of course, every man in Wyoming learned to ride, and Graham and his three brothers were no exception. But it had been a very, very long time since he'd saddled up in any sense of the word.

But today, though the lodge was a huge building, with dozens of places to which he could escape, he felt trapped. So he plucked his hat from the peg by the door and positioned it on his head. He didn't get many opportunities to wear a cowboy hat in Seattle, but here, he'd worn it every day. And he liked it.

The brim kept the snow off his face as he trudged down the path he'd shoveled everyday since moving in and toward the stables.

The stables were named DJ Riders, and Graham had no idea where it had come from. There were only three horses that had come with the property, and thankfully, the loft held enough hay to keep them fed for a while.

Graham went through the motions of feeding them, cleaning out their stalls, and making sure they had fresh water that hadn't frozen over. January in Wyoming wasn't for the weak-hearted, that was for sure, horse or human.

The chores done, Graham closed up the stables but turned away from the lodge up the lane. He had plenty of unpacking to do and no inclination to do it. Besides, it would keep, as he'd been living in the lodge for three days without the family pictures, all the dishes, or more than one towel. He'd survived so far, thanks to a four-wheel-drive vehicle and a pocketful of cash.

He wandered away from the stables, the barn, the rest of the outbuildings of the lodge. He passed a gazebo he hadn't even known existed until that very moment, and he wondered what else he'd find on this parcel of land he'd put his name on. And who knew what spring would bring?

Probably pollen and allergies, he thought, still not entirely happy to be back in Coral Canyon though he'd made the decision to leave his job in Seattle and settle back in his hometown.

The snow muted his footsteps and made it difficult to go very far very fast. Didn't matter. He had the whole day to do whatever he wanted. Tomorrow too. It wasn't until Monday that he'd have to put on a suit and start figuring out how to manage an energy company with over two hundred employees.

He approached another building, this one a bit different than the ones he'd seen before. He wasn't sure what it was, though it looked like a small cabin, with a stovepipe sticking out of the shingles on the roof. Did the lodge have a smaller place to live? Was this another guest area he could rent out?

He stepped closer and peered in the window, not seeing a door anywhere. The place was simply furnished and appeared to be one room with a door leading out of it on his right and into what he assumed was a bedroom.

A woman came out of the bedroom, buttoning her coat.

Graham yelped and backed up at the same time a dog put his front paws on the windowsill inside the house and started barking. And barking. And barking.

With his heart pounding and his adrenaline spiking out of control, Graham's brain didn't seem to be working properly. Therefore, he couldn't move. Didn't even think to move.

So he was still standing there like a peeping Tom when the woman lifted the window and said, "What are you doing here?" in a tone of voice that could've frozen the water into snow if the temperature hadn't already done it.

"I—I—" Graham stammered. "Who are you?"

She cocked her hip, and Graham noticed the long, honey-blonde hair as she threw it over her shoulder before folding her arms. She possessed a pretty face, with a sprinkling of freckles across her cheeks and nose. Her eyes could've been any color, as he was looking from the outside in and the light wasn't the same.

If he'd had to, he'd categorize them as dangerous, especially when they flashed lightning at him.

"I am the owner of this property," she said. "And you're trespassing."

Graham frowned, but at least his brain had started operating normally again. It was his pulse that was galloping now, wondering what he had to do to get invited in to find out what color those eyes were.

"Oh," he said. "I'm sorry. I thought this was my place. I just bought Whiskey Mountain Lodge." He waved in the general direction of the lodge, hoping it was the right way.

"The border is back there about a hundred yards," she said, still positioned like he might come at her through the window screen. "There's a fence."

"Maybe it's buried in all the snow." Because he had definitely not crossed a fence line. He might have become a city slicker but he still knew what a fence meant. "I'm Graham Whittaker."

A noise halfway between a squeak and a meow came from her mouth. Those eyes rounded, but he still couldn't tell what color they were. "Graham Whittaker?"

He tilted his head now, studying her. Because she knew him. No one spoke with that much surprise in their voice if they didn't know a person.

"Yes," he said slowly. "I'm...." He didn't know how to finish. Everyone in Coral Canyon knew his father had died. Everyone knew the Whittakers had come to mourn. He supposed everyone though they'd all left again, except for his mother and his youngest brother, Beau, who lived in town and worked as a lawyer.

But he didn't know what he was still doing in Coral Canyon, or why he felt the urge to explain it to this woman.

"Just a second." She slammed the window closed and moved away. Feeling stupid, Graham stood there in the snow, wondering what she was going to do. Half a minute later, the dog that had tried to rip his face off through the glass came bounding through the snow from the front of the house.

"Clearwater," the woman called after him, but the dog was either disobedient or didn't care. The blue heeler came right up to Graham and started sniffing him.

Graham chuckled and scratched the dog behind his ears. "Yeah, I've got a lab. You can probably smell 'im. Bear? His name's Bear."

The blonde woman came around the corner of the cabin, and she stopped much further away than her dog had. "Graham Whittaker." This time she didn't phrase it as a question, and a hint of a smile touched her lips. "You don't remember me, do you?"

Graham abandoned his administrations to the dog and took a step toward her, trying to place her. He thought he'd definitely remember someone as shapely as her, what with those long legs that curved into hips and narrowed to a waist, even in the black jacket she'd buttoned around herself.

He was about to apologize when the answer hit him full in the chest. "Laney Boyd?" He tore his eyes from hers to glance around the land, not that he could tell anything with the piles and piles of snow.

"Is this Echo Ridge Ranch?" he asked. He hadn't realized the lodge property butted up against the ranch where he'd spent time as a teenager. And without looking back at Laney, he knew he'd find a pair of light green eyes. Eyes that came to life when she was atop a horse. Eyes that had always called to him. Eyes that saw more than he'd ever wanted her to. Beautiful, light green eyes he wanted to get to experience again.

When he looked at her again, her grin had filled her whole face. "It's Laney McAllister now," she said, dashing every hope he had of rekindling an old friendship—and maybe making it into something more.

Which is stupid, he told himself as he chuckled and walked through the snow to give her a hug hello. *You just got your heart broken. No need to do it again.*

———

GRAHAM is available now in ebook, audiobook, and paperback!

The Marine's Marriage: A Fuller Family Novel - Brush Creek Cowboys Romance (Book 1): Tate Benson can't believe he's come to Nowhere, Utah, to fix up a house that hasn't been inhabited in years. But he has. Because he's retired from the Marines and looking to start a life as a police officer in small-town Brush Creek. Wren Fuller has her hands full most days running her family's company. When Tate calls and demands a maid for that morning, she decides to have the calls forwarded to her cell and go help him out. She didn't know he was moving in next door, and she's completely unprepared for his handsomeness, his kind heart, and his wounded soul. **Can Tate and Wren weather a relationship when they're also next-door neighbors?**

The Firefighter's Fiancé: A Fuller Family Novel - Brush Creek Cowboys Romance (Book 2): Cora Wesley comes to Brush Creek, hoping to get some in-the-wild firefighting training as she prepares to put in her application to be a hotshot. When she meets Brennan Fuller, the spark between them is hot and  instant. As they get to know each other, her deadline is constantly looming over them, and Brennan starts to wonder if he can break ranks in the family business. He's okay mowing lawns and hanging out with his brothers, but he dreams of being able to go to college and become a landscape architect, but he's just not sure it can be done. **Will Cora and Brennan be able to endure their trials to find true love?**

The Trooper's Treasure: A Fuller Family Novel - Brush Creek Cowboys Romance (Book 3): Dawn Fuller has made some mistakes in her life, and she's not proud of the way McDermott Boyd found her off the road one day last year. She's spent a hard year wrestling with her choices and trying to fix them, glad for McDermott's acceptance and friendship. He lost his wife years ago, done his best with his daughter, and now he's ready to move on. **Can McDermott help Dawn find a way past her former mistakes and down a path that leads to love, family, and happiness?**

The Detective's Date: A Fuller Family Novel - Brush Creek Cowboys Romance (Book 4): Dahlia Reid is one of the best detectives Brush Creek and the surrounding towns has ever had. She's given up on the idea of marriage—and pleasing her mother—and has dedicated herself fully to her job. Which is great, since

one of the most perplexing cases of her career has come to town. Kyler Fuller thinks he's finally ready to move past the woman who ghosted him years ago. He's cut his hair, and he's ready to start dating. Too bad every woman he's been out with is about as interesting as a lamppost—until Dahlia. He finds her beautiful, her quick wit a breath of fresh air, and her intelligence sexy. **Can Kyler and Dahlia use their faith to find a way through the obstacles threatening to keep them apart?**

The Paramedic's Partner: A Fuller Family Novel - Brush Creek Cowboys Romance (Book 5): Jazzy Fuller has always been overshadowed by her prettier, more popular twin, Fabiana. Fabi meets paramedic Max Robinson at the park and sets a date with him only to come down with the flu. So she convinces Jazzy to cut her hair and take her place on the date. And the spark between Jazzy and Max is hot and instant...if only he knew she wasn't her sister, Fabi.

Max drives the ambulance for the town of Brush Creek with is partner Ed Moon, and neither of them have been all that lucky in love. Until Max suggests to who he thinks is Fabi that they should double with Ed and Jazzy. They do, and Fabi is smitten with the steady, strong Ed Moon. **As each twin falls further and further in love with their respective paramedic, it becomes obvious they'll need to come clean about the switcheroo sooner rather than later...or risk losing their hearts.**

The Chief's Catch: A Fuller Family Novel - Brush Creek Cowboys Romance (Book 6): Berlin Fuller has struck out with the dating scene in Brush Creek more times than she cares to admit. When she makes a deal with her friends that they can choose the next man she goes out with, she didn't dream they'd pick surly Cole Fairbanks, the new Chief of Police.

His friends call him the Beast and challenge him to complete ten dates that summer or give up his bonus check. When Berlin approaches him, stuttering about the deal with her friends and claiming they don't actually have to go out, he's intrigued. As the summer passes, Cole finds himself burning both ends of the candle to keep up with his job and his new relationship. **When he unleashes the Beast one time too many, Berlin will have to decide if she can tame him or if she should walk away.**

Grab your favorite cup of cocoa or coffee and get comfortable, because you'll get a sweet, clean, and faith-filled romance in every book in the Christmas in Coral Canyon series. Join the Whittaker brothers - cowboy billionaires in Wyoming - as they build strong family bonds, fun holiday traditions, and relationships with the women who make them want to be better men.

GRAHAM (Book 1): Graham Whittaker returns to Coral Canyon a few days after Christmas—after the death of his father. He takes over the energy company his dad built from the ground up and buys a high-end lodge to live in— only a mile from the home of his once-best friend, Laney McAllister. They were best friends once, but Laney's always entertained feelings for him, and spending so much time with him while they make Christmas memories puts her heart in danger of getting broken again...

Go up the canyon to Brush Creek Ranch, where a community of retired rodeo cowboys are looking for love…

Brush Creek Cowboy (Book 1): He's a cowboy raising his son alone. She's a widow with a chocolate obsession. **Can Brush Creek cowboy Walker get over his losses and fears in order to build a future with Tess?**

About Liz

Liz Isaacson writes inspirational romance, usually set in Texas, or Wyoming, or anywhere else horses and cowboys exist. She lives in Utah, where she writes full-time, takes her two dogs to the park everyday, and eats a lot of veggies while writing. Find her on her website, along with all of her pen names, at feelgoodfictionbooks.com.